I0611937

Wise Parents, Happy Children

Holistic Intuitive Parenting
Loving Actions, Gentle process

Utasha. T

ZORBA BOOKS

ZORBA BOOKS

Publishing Services in India by Zorba Books, 2019

Website: www.zorbabooks.com
Email: info@zorbabooks.com

Copyright © **Utasha. T**

Print Book ISBN 978-93-88497-71-8
E-book ISBN 978-93-88497-72-5

All rights reserved. No part of this book may be reproduced or transmitted in any form or by any means, electronic or mechanical, except by a reviewer. The reviewer may quote brief passages, with attribution, in a review to be printed in a magazine, newspaper, or on the Web—without permission in writing from the copyright owner.

The publisher under the guidance and direction of the author has published the contents in this book, and the publisher takes no responsibility for the contents, it's accuracy, completeness, any inconsistencies, or the statements made. The contents of the book do not reflect the opinion of the publisher or the editor. The publisher and editor shall not be liable for any errors, omissions, or the reliability of the contents of the book.

Any perceived slight against any person/s, place or organization is purely unintentional.

Zorba Books Pvt. Ltd.(opc)
Gurgaon, INDIA

I dedicate this work to the Strength in Changing Seasons.

The loving relationships we share with Mother and Father Earth.

The contributor and leader in all of us,

and to the heartfelt home-maker in You Me and Us.

Utasha..

Signed from my heart to your's!

About the Author

Utasha's study is in Psychology and Holistic Healing living. And expertise in creative writing, she has certifications of childbirth educator, heal your life training and many more. However she was brought up in an aesthetic background with clothes and fashion shows, she blended her interests with learning about positive psychology, her belief is to envision and co create a world, in which, We live in a world of harmony and truth and nonviolence and understanding, wisdom and happiness and having compassion for our generation gap. Her hobbies include skin care, music, cooking, giving workshops on her topic of expertise. She believes once we find our unique calling or passion, we must nurture it and watch it grow into something fruitful and beautiful.

As my name is ut 'asha' which means hope, I add a small plea and wish for us, I hope we feel and honor the sacred unconditional love of life through our process Of becoming and feeling closer to our glorious true selves through the process of parenting and pregnancy.

Being a parent means to appreciate lifes effort to retouch, shape, a generation, and to re learn and grow in ways which suit and bring us joy.

Acknowledgements

Treat this book as your friend, as it has been my huge pleasure to write this book, and I have experienced such amazing growth through the process of writing and choosing harmonious content for the wholeness of the book.

I want to acknowledge so many people who helped me work through this book right till the last passage. Who motivated me when I felt like giving up as this was my first project. I am grateful to this beautiful universe for helping those who have a sincere desire to share wisdom that enriches our society, even an inch.

I want to acknowledge my publisher Zorba Books for being understanding, my family for being super understanding and caring, my friends for always motivating me to do my best,. Myself for the persistence to see the book through. I want to thank the artists for the art work they did for the book, I would also like to acknowledge my cappa education which helped me with better understanding of child development. I would like to thank my own courage to study what I liked and for finding the best bits to put together for you. I want to acknowledge every person, who inspired and motivated me through it all.

Thank you

Introduction

When one wants to feel close to their child in any way, first it is essential to feel close to your own self, grow and relearn evolve and then you have so much to share that it brims both of you with love, joy, happiness, and grace. That is when you know parenting is developing into a blooming, kind and lifelong partnership.

"Learning is never meant to be forceful, or feel tedious or lacking interest learning is meant to feel joyful and exciting and challenging and choicefull, and sometimes even deepening".

Trees are Earths endless effort to speak to the listening heaven

-Rabindranath Tagore

"Protection and nurturing are natural quality action of all parents, it all depends the way we choose to protect and nurture that defines us as parents."

Something about the *kind and caring* world and, the unfathomable wonder full universe is so pure, beautiful and wonderful that it connects you with the right people/ resources/information you require for your growth, and happiness, All we need is Gratitude Patience and courage to walk on our unique journey's and embrace and acknowledge our unique calling so in this process, have huge amounts of *Karuna* (compassion for yourself) and ability to make right decisions for yourself, and in joy and care for others who are with you going through the process with you, Life can be a little difficult and is, but remembering our Unity diversity, saves us from much drama & returning to grace is inviting the experience with ease, trust, preparation and happiness.

Treat this book as your comforting and enriching companian, some nuggets to, as to why are you writing/ sharing this book?!

We share something everyday, either through the medium of technology, or through so many other ways, we all desire to reach out authentically to each other in some way, and in the larger sense we are part of the larger world, so it is so important to know and realize what we are sharing, what is the quality of that sharing, whom is it impacting, and what is the need for it to be in highlight, that makes the sharing impactful and wonderful.

When I was in my early teens and 20's as a young adult, who was sensitive and never wanted to settle for less, and also a little confused about my life path what I should do, how I should take my responsibilities, but my seeking was very authentic and it became into this book, and development and finding of a beautiful talent in me. I believe we all should have that support starting from the time we start learning about life, and to begin with to be aware of this most important part of our lives parenting and pregnancy.

My first book was just going to be a compilation of plain Recipes and poems,(my love for cooking) and quotes But, fortunately as my background, in college was of Arts and Sociology and Psychology got me interested to write on parenting and pregnancy.

However I realized its not just theory that children and students will need in education it is the practical application of what will help them in life, its not psychological or just cramming information hunger that will feed anyone's heart it is emotional bonding and connection with our true joy, while it brightens our lives with a caring education that is good for the 'heart' mind and our spirit. It can brighten someone else's life, this is what will make us more whole as a society.

And as I found my gentle motivation day by day to begin gently with This book is my 'time energy effort excitement' to bring Hope and grace in the so often race of life, in the process of Parenting and Pregnancy.

So, do and be open to love, learn, laugh forgive, share, cry, enjoy, play as the process is meant to be caring, insightful, and friendly.

I have written out of moments of inspiration, delight and growth learning my lessons as authentically as I could by practicing mindfulness, and still learning, on my journey. And when everyday is feeling Like a fresh day and not a drag even if you are doing something small *yet meaningful to you it makes all the difference.*

Sometimes destiny takes us to make us our most authentic selves your delightfully welcome as you explore, the most important Real and a little sensitive area of life called parenting and pregnancy.

Spend one month with your family, and you will know how close you are To enlightenment'

Well what he meant is the maximum growth happens through this area of life.

As it directly connects and aligns life to life,
Heart to heart,
Walk to walk
And development to development
And growth to gratitude to giving.
And this does not need a Wifi
Just a willing involved fresh insightful
heart and mind
To evolve with the beautiful direction
Which is holistic gentle and caring.

And also,
Age to age
Generation to generation,
And there in that gap
We can
experience,
Respect compassion and real care for
Each other and life just as it is.

But in pregnancy you are the heart beat and
the baby is the developing seed,
Seed (the purity and organic potential
Divine Seed– Self enriched embracing divine.
Your emotions and devotions,
Habits and perceptions,
Of the world,
Whether it comes out of the seed of love, or
seed of fear,
Is
Going to affect the developing seed.
Hence relying and asking for all the support,
during this process
should feel safe.

This book is not a medical intervention or any other kind of intervention, or giving promises of cure which could replace medical or psychological or any other kind of help please don't substitute it for what is needed to get done, this book definitely gives Wisdom, knowledge and important information to make the pregnancy and parenting an easy and happier and a wiser one (psst) what so many parents want for their children, This book may talk about the journey of becoming a mom or a parent and much deeper but, it is always your Intuition that provokes you to learn and listen deeper.

Enjoy the journey!

Message to the reader

Having read couple of books myself I realized what is means to actually invest time in reading, it could mean differently for every person.

I realized what it means to be a 'mindful reader means to not read recklessly but read as if there is something new to learn. If you are reading in a group or a in a book club read and discuss with everyone in a non-judgmental manner

Your reading is what catches your attention, it does not need to catch attention of another person the same manner.

What really touches you, passages that move you are what you need to read often at a certain time of your life. The author is writing from another 'space time' maybe a different time zone than you, so read logically and also imbibe what you like/need and do Comment on the Authors page about their impact on you. And also see what they are essentially trying to convey from what they are sharing. Gladly share it with other readers when you feel like!

When your mind wanders, gently usher yourself back to the text and keep going.

If you've forgotten the last passage you read, you can always go back and read it again.

Or don't. There's value in a bit of uncertainty, in finding peace within ambiguity.

When you start spacing out or losing interest don't force yourself to complete reading

You can read it another time when you Intend or feel like.

Contents

Gentle Chapter 1

Affirming and shaping a conscious
Joyous Mindest, You me and us

♫♫♪♪ ♡

Before you speak
Letting our words pass
Through
Three gates
Is it necessary
Is it kind
Is it true?

Bringing balance and harmony in our lives
Can we bring it in?

Karuna

Karuna is the quality of giving and receiving. Strong social relationships, including sharing and mutual help, Rev up the immune system keeps us healthy and contributes to a peaceful life.

> How you practice karuna in your life.
> Get involved in spiritual community.
> Take up a hobby
> Become a volunteer
> Develop family traditions
> Eat together
> Reach out to someone.

A family that involves themselves in the quality of Karuna experience mutual growth, sharing and compassion.

Sringara or love

Sringara is love and Love is freeing and healing, There are different types of love from Vatsaya a mothers love, to Maîtri love of friends and platonic the Pure love between brother sisters and family and friends even relatives. Then there is love for nation, then also the universal love and reverence that one can feel for all creatures. This has less ego and more care.

How you practice Sringara in your family and community allow love to breathe and come in give love space and time. Celebrate love Contemplate on loving actions.

Hasya

Hasya is laughter laughter strengths the immune and nervous system and preserves good health and keeps bay illnesses laughter even controls blood pressure and heart diseases. Such as obesity, smoking, and excessive intake of saturated fats.

Hence,
Practice hasya when
You are involved in something
That is consuming
Bring laughter in that activity.
Embrace more cheerfulness in your life
Enjoy little moments and things of life.
Listen to laughter of babies and coming from
school children.
And even elders.

Adhbuta

Wonder develops from no judgement towards lifes experiences and being in awe of the moment. Welcome Wonder in your life it brings wisdom of even Ageing gracefully.

Be alone in silence for 10-15 minutes per day. Enjoy a walk amongst trees and gardens Look at the beautiful flowers Plant seeds and trees Set apart time to enjoy beauty.

Also this makes us closer to realise where we are being manupilating or manupilated, or where we actually want to Be, love is keeping ourselves protected from manupilation at all costs and being heart smart.

All the above qualities we need help in bringing awareness love and wisdom into our lives.

Maintaining balance in daily life

I realized how important it is to not lose your balance in everyday life, spirituality teaches us to listen to our inner voice and bring out our authentic selves more gracefully in every area of our lives, well obviously achieving balance is a unique process for everyone, all areas of our lives require our gentle nurturing support and attention to not keep them from getting dead or drying to keep them happy fresh and alive we can intend to cultivate more good qualities and weed out the guilt negativity and anger and plant more equality love and compassion, well how did I meet my inner voice?

Just like the seasons every season can make us feel either dead or alive, Excited or happy, it's could also mean the way we respond.

Respecting my relationship with mother earth, or if doing my best.

Parents do their best by helping their children have a good relationship with the earth, our earth is huge, we do house it city it, and work on it, sometimes against it and sometimes for it when we evolve we work with it and we help ourselves and earth at the same time by taking care how we use, treat and work against it or for it. Below are some activities to do good for each other and our planet earth.

Is reminding them that wisdom lies in little thoughtful loving deeds.

Switching off lights when not in use is being caring and 'wise' and being aware of litle things during the day, small gestures, donating something to someone in need boiling only as much water as you need (we double the energy for that purpose) Do not throw out re useable paper products.

Opting for electronic banking or billing. Discover your left over medicines so they can be distributed. Try horseback riding or walking. Wash your car with recycled water, Choose cooking oil in glass bottles.

Own bank with love and affection, then shine on others.

Buying an electronic car. Doing a spring cleaning often to protect their sensuality and revere life. Opt for slow food/ fast food. Watering your garden in the evening. Introducing sexual education and environmental education in school. Take a shower than a bath. Cover soil to protect it from evaporation and weed growth. Quit smoking.

Nurture their own unique creativity and individuality and never let that be sacrificed.

This department is flexible and we allow our children to grow find their interest, explore them responsibly and achieve! Following a unique talent doing more of what brings you happiness.

Did you know?

Evolution Facts

The first sign of pregnancy is when you miss your period.

At birth a baby girl already has about one million (eggs) ova, by the time she reaches puberty, the rare 200,000 to 400,000 of them left. Still this Is more than enough, Because each month an ovum is released on rare occasion are two ovum released which is the result of identical twins.

- A scorpion gives birth to 75,000 eggs.
- A sea horse has, 1000 babies.
- A salmon dark has 2-5 babies.
- An octupus has 20,000 to 100,000 eggs.
- A sea turtle has 50,2000 eggs
- A clown fish has 100,1000 eggs.
- A blue whale has, 2-3 kids every 2-3 years.
- Octopus lays, thousands of eggs but only 1 or 2 octupus actually survive.
- This just means that we already have a healthy environment and how much
- Effect the environment has on our species.

The gift of gab

The womans tounge is
Directly connected to her fetus and
her abdomen
Hence to take care of that,
And be conscious of that
With words,
In eating habits and speaking.
Is the most important
Task ever.
Hence, nourish and take care of that temple,
don't let any,
Harsh chemicals, of this world,
Affect that beautiful throat,
Keep it beautiful, and
Fresh.
And kind and honored

I respect my voice
Its accent, its quality and texture
just the way it is and the way it is not.
Its uniqueness and its uniqueness.
That is beautiful, the gift of gab is precious

My true inner voice	Voices of should be's
feels nourishing alive and true quick in tune with how I feel about a situation feels emotionally securing outgoing positive optimistic True inner voice never manipulates our nature Tires to change us But tries to be uplifting Keeping others in mind Caring Gentle and Assertive.	Feels Fake comfort Pleasing Delays inconsistently Attracts more painful experiences And learning through struggle. Keeping only self in mind Lonliness Should be Sounds like Its not even my voice it's the voice of fear

Meditate

A gentle affirmation

Letting there be a graceful and beautiful shower of celeberation and joy in my part of the earth and my family community to yours with the news of a new seed being sown which needs sunlight of warmth of parents, moonlight of surrender and faith and hope, that feels fresh and heeds to a fit and fabulous beginning.

One thing we must remind ourselves often and our children is: that they are 'good enough. Smart enough caring enough intelligent enough giving enough, and so are you, Parenting is a skill developed with experience enrichment and learning wisely, which requires nurturance, time and quality, just like a pregnancy with quality, even parenting with quality requires, your attention care and love. And enough ness.

Our biggest fear is not that we are inadequate but we are powerful and beyond measure. Only, in enough ness, do we find, and can create, the heart- fullness and mindfulness a person who does not feel 'enough ness'

will struggle, to create it, because, they don't know how to fill their cup, well nor did we, once upon a time that is why wherever you are in your life journey, its your own experience, that has been your teacher, and your guide, because in our own unique experience do we grow and learn and can contribute in some way.

What is 'being conscious'?

According to me if you are conscious you genuinely make the effort to be being present without your own agendas and that is truly the biggest heartful, giving and you feel fresh and alive. It might feel the most natural way to be, but we usually lose flow of it often, because of impatience and worry. It is not difficult to remember this, as this is how we all are really made naturally until we start believing negatively. All babies are born happy perfect and beautiful but to have a healthy pregnancy we can consciously shape and improve ourselves our environment and life to welcome nourish embrace and care for ourselves and the baby. The sunlight is everywhere, and it shows us the possibility of a good harvest just the effort to water and plant the rightful deeds are In our hands, In this chapter we will read some meaningful and sensible poetry,which will remind you to take some time in the day to reflect whether you are really happy, in so many colorful aspects of our lives. Reading heartfelt poetry during pregnancy or in our lives enriches our inner self and we also realize our faint oneness with life.

The gifts of living consciously as the spiritual masters have been saying since centuries are enormous, there is more vitality inner strength ability to handle with with strength, grace gratitude and courage.

Ability to choose responses than be enslaved with reactions being a parent/ mother is learning about strengths you didn't know you had, and dealing with Fears compassionately you didn't know existed.

What an unconscious day might look like:

You consume packaged or fast food.
You act rush and pressured.
You listen without really paying attention.
You feel fatigue without doing any invigorating physical work.
You feel stuck and unfulfilled.
You fail to stand up for yourself
You behave like a people pleaser.

Pause for a while, and notice and reflect what kind of a day are you having, what is the quality of it?

How can I recognize my inner self from ego?

One example of difference between inner self and ego is the night and morning both are sweet, only we become bitter.- Said by Sadhguru and is an insightful way to recognize when your inner self is shutting down to the sweetness of living life.

You will read many affirmations in the book, in different contexts, I have written them so you can affirm, and bring in added positivity to your experience..(they are all original and made by the author)

What is affirmation?

Affirmation is a technique through which we can get influenced by a better thought a wiser perspective, and a better way of doing and being so we can achieve our results with less stress, ease, joy, and wonder in life.

Remember, affirmation just needs your side. You need to be on your side to affirm. No matter what you have experienced in your life, positive thinking can bring you good results.

Repeat these affirmations in the book, though the word affirmation has evolved from French psycho-therapist Emile Coue. His affirmation to his patients- every day I am getting better and better. Was given to his patients to repeat in the morning and evening in order to alter or affect the unconscious thoughts. Everyone is unique, hence everyones affirmation is unique.

The first time I ever used an affirmation was I learnt from a spiritual class of louise hay ' Heal your life' I was aware of this concept but as I explored it I realized it works only when you are feeling Fit and you know that what you want will be A hit.

Hit= harmony in time.
Fit- fresh in truth.

In changing seasons and for a 100 reasons I can choose to respond with love or with fear in every season and for every reason I can choose whom where how to evolve in all different seasons shows the beautiful variety of nature and I am grace in the changing seasons for all the right reasons.

IF you hang out with chickens you will pluck, if you hang out with pigs you will grunt. If you hang out with eagles you fly, the company we keep. makes a lot of difference at all times.

When we are affirming we remember the eternal nature of life that we cant control, yet we are part of and experience the consequences of all our deeds I remember this short prayer ***I am responsible for what I see, what I hear and what I do and everything that I experience is what I have asked for or invited at some level*** and in this remembering I am free from blame complain and too many expectations.

I was blessed to attend affirmation class and learn about affirmations they work really well, if you learn to couple them with confidence and reflection even for 10-15 minutes in a day in an overwhelming day with confidence and reflection even for 10-15 minutes really during your pregnancy. So,consider the good thoughts in this book as affirmations, you can reflect on one or two and see how it affects you positively. Mostly the good effect of a positive affirmation is a change in behavior, character, destiny, and the quality of life.

A loving spirit of a parent helps the child to remember his or her own greatness, authentically.

Ease- effortless allow surrender embrace

The best medicine in the world is a mothers kiss. Finding ease means not fighting with the flow. And taking charge of your own moods mannerisms and matters. Than projecting them on others.

I respect the wisdom of my being affirmation for medical ease I go through my pregnancy process with ease, grace and effortless enthusiasm I let go of perfection, and embrace the spontaneity beauty of everyday living.

I balance my rest and activity and this increases my physical and health full energy. Reeducating my mind and body to learn to trust the divine intelligence within me and in nature, I will make amazing choices throughout my pregnancy.

I balance my sit, stand, move and rest sitting for too long depletes our energy, hence gentle movement is helpful.

My anxiety eases with the knowledge that there are really good professionals out there who will help me with this process and in this knowledge I surrender to uplift my baby to the best experience in the womb, And for the outside of it in the world, down.

A togetherness 'thought'

Our love together is giving birth to another, consciously and lovingly welcoming in heartfullness and mindfulness and in learning to relate to each other and life more sensitively, sensibly and joyously.

A small prayer for the little one

I pray that the little one can sense with the amount of care joy, and arrangements we make how much they are wanted, I hope he or she Remember the language of belonging and love as they are developing, dreaming and moving in my womb, I hope he or she remembers that I am also part of the greater womb and can welcome them to come and dance enjoy and create, As she comes and makes this world a better place their actions, love, and light the best gifts we give to the little one are the ones which we give ourselves—connection, happiness, simplicity, and goodness.

I hope they remember that the temple of our hearts and families have been waiting for this new member with all our might, love, and eagerness.

I hope you enjoy the strength grace and beauty of every age.

A true learner or a person who understands maturely knows that, wisdom is to be remembered celebrated and respected, not learnt or overshadowed by fears worries and Imaginings. Remember means to make a member again.

Did you know?

Do you know eating under the moonlight and sunlight during your pregnancy is an excellent way to attract and be around natural light, which is actually good for you, your womb, and your life force why?

Natural light decreases the seasonal affective disorder (SAD) and makes you healthier happier. Do you know watering plants and watching them grow, and keeping a home plant, is also beneficial during pregnancy. Why? Because touching natural materials is naturally calms the nerves!

Do you know, eating out every day can seem fun but actually it should only be done only in moderation.

Do you know accepting help from another community, enriches both together.

Do you know, seclusion and isolation were ways to connect and relax from the world, These days it's more fun to connect within communities. Groups, and workshops, Occasionally and why? Because lonliness and seclusion are aspects of fear. And togetherness and communities are source of strength and protection.

Did you know that meditating some minutes during your day can heal and relax your sensory mind and nerves even more?

What pregnancy guides us towards is an aspect of embracing 'healthy pleasure' noticing goodness hope and lovearound trying staying away from substance abuse, spending time in nature. This is not a regime for a healthy life, but embracing healthy pleasure makes us more 'wiser' and happier.

- Share
- Harmoniously
- Aware
- Read/realise
- Enrich

Taking responsibility for your process

Pregnancy that is initiated with unawareness or right age or taking under considerations all factors important for the pregnancy can lead to abortion or miscarriages, because if one isnt involved in the pregnancy fully, you have to measure and check your availability needs and divine timing for your pregnancy, that all needs will be met. You are in gratitude and peace and you feel truly for your heart to commit to this pregnancy. Why take a half hearted approach? If your heart is not in it, why go ahead with the process?

For too many women pregnancy and birth is something that happens to them rather than something they set out consciously and joyfully to do themselves. Then only one can take responsibility for it. So, intention- I will nurture the sensible and wonderful seed of pregnancy when I am ready for it.

Written on 2017 October

The gift of good decisions, rises with those who have love and compassion.

Good decisions come from

- Clarity
- Equality
- Relaxation
- Intuition and a little bit of intellect
- Gut feeling
- Humbleness and happiness
- Wholeness
- Trustworthy advice
- Assertion
- Love
- Deserveability.

Not so good decisions spring from

- Delusion
- Ego
- Inequality
- Hatred
- Intrusions
- Malice advice
- Fear

Love is all accepting and knowing, that is the gift of love and being loved.

Everyone experiences love in their own way in the most truest form it is unconditional and guarding and caring and freedom.

Have patience because living with the heart requires us to live with humbleness, enrichment risking our truth.

Affirming my good decisions

I bless my good decisions with truest wish and highest love and my highest love knowing every decision has a consequence I try my best to make my decisions with stability, love, keeping others in mind and my truest realization. Om namah peace.

Purity of the senses

The first and the last thing in the process of attainment of good health and youth is purity of our senses. Sensing is an activity of every living being. Every action movement has its sense. Mainly the purity in thought and purity in action are included.

- Sense of feeling.
- Sense of perception.
- Sense of touching
- Sense of tasting
- Sense of movement
- Sense of living
- Sense of feeling.

Let's look at a baby, you look at a baby and you see the purity in all these senses. Their senses start getting getting dull when they are overstimiulated, or one isnt happy. With the world recovering from its negativity, however, it takes lot of discipline, stability, and sense to keep the purity of senses alive, in the way we relate to life, What is the best is Heartfullness and Mindfulness.

We can perhaps learn from the book, "significant world of insignificant weeds".

"The value of good health precedes over anything else, because only with good health, can we make a healthy happy life."

When we live a life of balance we recognize and have a gentle ability to say stop to excess and yes to balance that is when we tap into real Living. Rest is all indulgence.

Lets look at the positives of every culture

- Every culture promotes care of the mother in the best way possible.
- Every culture wants to ward off Evil from the Baby.
- Every culture tries their best to strive to keep their dignity and beauty.
- Every culture believes in a higher power, Astrology covers moon?
- Every culture has access to beautiful names for baby.
- Some cultures believe in eating certain animals helps to have a healthier baby.

Hence finding harmony should not be difficult because every cultures intention is good, if we could promote and only feed the good in the culture, we could tarnish evil from cultures. Starts with our beliefs that is why having a little flexibility, in every view point is so essential.

I intend to take the wisest from my culture and imbibe the best from it, in truth we are all equal and loved. in the eyes of our creator.

Gentle affirmation: I intend to take the wisest from all culture ...

Pregnancy practices throughout the world				
Turkey	Pregnancy	fasten hair	Postpartum.	What would you imbibe from this culture?
	LOOK at the moon and beautiful people.	Unlock windows.	May dress the baby in a sand filled diaper.	
	Smell roses	Feed birds	May bath the baby in salt water.	
	Eat apples, green plums, and grapes.	Have a woman who had easy birth rub her back.	Mother and baby not allowed for forty days.	
	Look at bears, camels, and monkeys.	Jump down from a high spot.		
	Eat fish rabbit sheeps head, or chew gum.			
	Eat hot bitter or spicy foods.			

Pregnancy practices throughout the world

East Indian	Pregnancy viewed as normal.	Isolated due to the impurity of birth.	Needs to remain warm.
	Physical activity is generally not limited.	Cry and may vocalize Men generally not at the delivery.	Bleeding may be seen just as beneficial it purifies the uterus.
	Twins may be viewed as unlucky.		May not shower.
			Eats cool foods.
			Consumption of milk, ghee butter some kind of fish encouraged.
Latina America.	Should drink chamomile tea	Inactivity results in the loss of amniotic fluid, and sticky baby.	Discouraged from taking a shower for several days.
	Wear a red string around the abdomen		May believe breastfeeding prevents pregnancy.
			Medications may be seen as dangerous and may be avoided.

Pregnancy practices throughout the world			
Hindu	Sacraments carried about in the second or third month, and between fifth to eight month. After the sacrament in the seventh month, the woman is expected to rest. Strict vegetarians. Male babies preferred Prefer female care providers.	Father touches babys lips with a gold spoon or ring dipped in honey. Modesty is important. The balance of hot vs cold foods. Ceremonies performed for a stillborn.	Naming sacrament happens 10-12 days A welcoming ceremony is performed. A dot behind the baby's ear wards of evil. The om symbol may be placed around the mothers neck or babys neck.

Pregnancy practices throughout the world

OrthodoxJewish.	May not prepare for the baby by purchasing baby related items. Should not reveal the baby's name.	Husband may not see the genital area watch the birth. May keep pregnancy quiet.	Breastfeeding considered for over 5 years.
Sikhism	Every child has a divine spark of the creator.	Family encouraged to meditate and pray. Mother will try to meditate. Shaving is discouraged. boys commonly have a last of or middle name of Kaur. Hair not cut a few days after birth. Breastfeeding encouraged.	

Gentle thinker

I think that religious customs have their own say and power and roots already set, but they can be flexible to good change, as some religious Beliefs are practicing favoritism imbalance and denying wholeness. None of them are bad. What matters is what we follow does not harm anyone purposely, and is good for all, in some care always wins over too much restriction or no joy in pregnancy. They do exist, and each to their own!

If you are allowed to explore your own way of living, without harming any life, and have freedom of choice to what to believe in goodness as it is, before complaining, and be in gratitude for the harmony and Wholeness you have created and have, and work on making a solid truthful foundation for it to sustain.

And notice if the behavior of some other cultures start influencing your behavior especially when it is NOT YOU.

To be yourself Without being heavily influenced is the best and wisest way....

The best kind of parenting teaches a child how to meditate and try to find their truth and live a truthful and kind Lifestyle and life.And stay flexible with religious dogma.

Basically what feels right is right for you and what feels not right is not. Right?

1. *How will you bring up your children?*

2. *And what are you influenced by?*

3. How flexible can you be?

4. What you cant replace?

'Your children are not your children
They are the sons and daughters of lifes longing
for itself.
They come through you but not from you.
You can strive to be like them, and show them
your best quality for them to imbibe from you.'

Inspired form the prophet book.
By kahlil Gibran
–Margret sanger

Keeping the strength the soil and soul of marriage, the inner and outer strength let's first look at the nature of the daughter a girl is like her own kind of shrub, flower or tree, first she is planted in her parent's home, then she gracefully shifts as she grows up, and then she has to learn to be a parent/mother one day so instead of just being planted, (the passive receiver) the woman has to be a giver to herself and her future family by consciously planting the seed of maturity and growth, and putting her own seeds of responsibility and if she is taught by her parents from the beginning how to be a proactive planter in a loving way, she will move beautifully into the next home and will be an asset not a liability. So she learns to plant goodness, love, community, and happiness its safe for a daughter to be a gentle offerer Offering kindness to herself and the relationship never over giving or rejecting what the son has to give, but adding on to that, when she becomes too passive she cant receive the offering beautifully and lovingly. Wherever she goes and receive proactively as well. Every good relationship needs a gentle effort of everyday to look fresh and happy and stable.

One day, someone asked Buddha

What is the difference between I like you and I love you?

Buddha replied gracefully when you like something you instantly pluck it, but when you love someone you water it daily.

Example of periods which every woman experiences.

A woman has a 3-4 day in a Month in which the rest of the days she is working on building her self esteem, when she is ovulating or in mensuration the entire focus goes into the abdomen area, but when her self esteem is good and well nourished she wont have to worry about the health of her abdomen. when we understand that the gap given to us between the time of our next period is the time to build our strength and self esteem even more we understand the wonder tenderness of being a woman.

Affirmation for parent

I will see through my childs growing phases with patience and gentleness. Ill learn to be gentle with my growing children.
We intend to see through our childs blooming with awe, patience, and gentleness. It

feels good to be discerning and helpful to my children'

Take out this time to build my social relationships, strength and outer beauty.

Those 3 days are enough to focus on inner beauty, and paying attention to your body's needs more sensitively.

I am bleeding out stuff which my body does not need.

I am light and graceful in all tasks I do.

We women are all different, hence the wonder of being a woman is

- Wow
- Woman of wisdom
- To women of wishful thinking.

Women who practise wishful thinking (which means only fantasy and instant gratification, and less connected to reality) are just accumilating more and more without having the courage to be practical and wise in daily life' that is truly a balanced mature girl who bases her worth on what truly matters.

For example giving in to addictions, or temporary pleasures, these are transient, instead a woman can spend that time in polishing her self esteem and graceful mannerisms.

We can be both, however we are all different our period cycles aren't same, we are all unique with unique features and unique details so the kindest affirmation could be to support each other than exploit or Berete each other, to build a bond and friendship and build a circle of support care and friendship.

Affirmation for womanhood

I am developing consciously and beautifully
as a woman.
I am loving and kind to other women.

I am seeing these roles from the 'eyes' of under-standing, rather than eyes of what we get accustomed to seeing and interpreting what a stereotypical son or daughter looks like.

Do you know in certain countries its important to have a son, well this kind of partiality should not make any sex feel inferior or not worthy, but to treat both of them as worthy, treating any child as useless demeans their potential and can make them feel they are not wanted.

Useless

You are useless, you don't matter.
'You don't do enough'

What we are saying is, you aren't living up to my expectations of how you should be today. And you don't matter.

We are trying to motivate the child but aren't finding the right words to do so, and this obviously creates friction where there can be a possibility of harmony and understanding.

'A gentle society will equally motivate the childs effort more than his IQ, but also not forget to motivate the latter.'

More gentler way to say it, "I see you are doing the best you are doing and let me know how I can help you."

In the perspective of mothers and elders as well, when we stop treating them as commodities, we can remember them, as having a life and dignity of their own, which means we don't own our mothers, mothers and women all of them need value, appreciation, acknowledgement for the unconditional love they give us that's all they need. When we gently realise this, we stop seeing getting old as ugly or boring or lonely or sad, we look forward to today and don't fear 'tommorow' our beliefs about Aeging are embedded in us since such a long time.

What is essential is to realise never to fear old age, again we carry these beliefs over time in our hearts and minds and it always takes time To let go but what matters Is, we remember that aeging gracefully means I have tried my best to live every situation and event in my life with the best possible response I could find, instead of being carried away by the moments energy or got angry, fearful and acted impulsively, this sends a message to my body and mind, that "*I have nothing to fear, when I m being my truest me at a moment*" & *I tuned into the bigger picture Gently.*

Affirmation- *My biology is unravelling the way its meant to and my grattitude stays youthful and joyful.*

Gratitude poetry reflective page

Gift and gratitude for Elders

The wisdom of their wrinkles
To the sun in their smiles
Elders shine with the unity
Useful just as they are
With the wisdom in their being.
Of
Possibility
Of a
More holistic world.
Their experience is a gift,
Their name will become a memory
and their wisdom and unconditional love
Will seldom be forgotten.

Write down 5 qualities you admire in elders, and also in yourself as an adult.

1.

2.

3.

4.

5.

6.

The gift of youth and individuality

Youth is you offering understanding
truth harmony
When you offer understanding truth harmony
You are offering
Your youthful energy in the most graceful
way possible
Which,
Does help you see situations from a wiser
perspective
And Kinder heart.

Write down 5 qualities you admire In yourself as youth or when you were young

1.

2.

3.

4.

5.

Start with what you know, mature, according to nature, let destiny do the rest'- Chaung Tzu.

These days the youth is quite cooperative, with learning new and more compassionate and wise ways of learning, someone just has to believe in them

The gift of Presence and Reunion

We are in each other's
Forests, lives, moments,
Reasons, Seasons, days, pace, culture,
exchanges,
Events, memories, life, thoughts,
Hearts, space.
yet why to still fight?
Isn't that a thought
Worth pondering about?

'Life is not meant to be thought about continually, but to be experienced joyfully simply and greatfully'

Insight: Giving and receiving both should feel Good to the Giver and receiver

Write down 5 qualities you love about others in your life

1)

2)

3)

4)

5)

6)

Written on 2018 June

The role of good habits and self love. Good habits are essential part of adding on to self love because, good habits are healing and becoming in tune with your true self's needs.

Even if anyone else does not get it you have to try to be true to what you know, when you realize and recognize it. And embrace it that is when it becomes a healing habit. Which is good for your mind body and self.

To live in a kind, beautiful crime free, world, we need no perfection, but strength to help each other for each other!

"A habit eventually ends up either making a character of wisdom, or a foolish character."

Take time to rebuild and redefine your vision every day of the week. How many qualities of this parent do you genuinely try to inculcate everyday in your authentic honesty embrace your healing habit.

What is not a healing or a good habit?

Any habit which brings you tension, anger upset dishonor is a habit which is not good for you and is good inches away.

Habits you can afford to have	Habits you cannot afford to have
Daily routine of Healthy eating Greatfullness Habit of avoiding phones and other communication objects when spending time with loved ones.	Smoking: smoking reduces O2 supply to the baby by causing constrictions of the vessels in the placenta. Alcahol cigerette smoking contains nicotine and carbon monooxide which are poisionus for fetal growth.
Habit of praying trusting in higher power Habit of enjoying the moment Habit of being true to your word as much as you can. Habit of being proactive.	Too much tv addiction: screen staring can hamper the growth of your brain, that is why whenever I was also writing this book, I would take constant breaks from the screen, and do daily tasks, or connect with nature. Obsession either with self or with another or an object. Habit of perfection or performing Worrying. Complaining too much.
If you have any of the above traits Increase and inculcate them more in your life.	If you have any of the above habits, please correct them immediately as we all know the horrible effects they have can have on the developing child.

Message to the Reader

This chapter formed very thoughtfully and naturally and why I call this chapter You me and us is because we are all different yet we meet at one common place our humanity, right? As It was the first chapter, I wanted the introduction to introduce the reader into the wisdom teaching of Buddhism which we can apply in our daily lives while writing this chapter I realized since it is the introduction, let me make it easily Digested thankfully I added these amazing teachings of Buddhism which means compassion (karuna) and maitry (friendship) written from this amazing book on community building called Happy Street context of becoming a parent in the future and if a parent is reading this they can remember what it means to add spirituality and sensitivity in daily life in some manner. I am very great full to leaving habits which didn't suit me and now my life feels a lot more peaceful and happier than before hence I mentioned the importance of good habits and imbibing kind self talk.

Questions to ask yourself, for conscious living.

- How charged was your phone today? Did you actually use it for conscious social texting or rubbish or gibberish?

- How many lights did you use today are you aware of misuse of it?

- What good decision did you take in the week that you are proud of?

- Which cultural practices have you seen your community practicing are you in agreement of them?

- How much did you really need the drive today? Did you really go somewhere important? Are you aware the earth is heating up because of harmful gases from cars. Just being aware, and teaching our children the same will make a less corrupted more healthier world and you me and us.(not saying driving is bad, but moderation is always helpful)

Quote 2 ponder: Only in personal balance and happiness can We contribute beautifully and successfully to community health beauty or balance or maybe the other way around but they do compliment each other.

Notes

1. What were some of the favourite lines from this chapter. How did it make you Feel?

_____

_____

_____

_____

_____

_____

_____

_____

_____

2. What insights did you receive to make your experience more enriching and meaningful?

_____

_____

_____

_____

_____

_____

_____

_____

_____

Blessed Chapter 2

Welcoming and making a loving *Space for your Baby, Neighbours of the heart*

Garden:

Acronym of	G	Growing
	a	and
	r	receiving
	d	daily
	e	enthusing
	n	nurturing

Relationship gardens

Our relationship is like a gardener if conditions are right, one's blooming and growth is healthy and happy. My home is protected peaceful and a paradise to rejuvenate and retreat to.

Throughout this chapter we will refer to how to have a ease and effortless pregnancy so this chapter hosts information for home changes to make referring to welcoming the baby and creating safe and caring surroundings even for the baby's size and access safety. I really enjoyed writing this chapter and I moved through writing I realized that everyone has their own unique home style, and here we can find even more harmony and gratitude for each other. *Our home is part of a city a city is part of a country and a country part of a continent and a continent part of the beautiful earth, so our home is the loving balm and closeness we feel with each other and life,* some we feel very close to, some we feel not so close, but here we can choose what suits us and be happy.

A home is not a home, without gentle familiarity, caring actions, heartfelt honesty, and a blanket full of wisdom and grace.

Simplicity is the best policy, a home reflects an individual's inner being to a large degree, and the way we maintain a home's energy defines what we most want in our lives, hence upgrading and evolving here keeping qualities of love, care equality, peace surrender hope in mind create a sanctuary for us to find our center.

Home is truly , Heaven of my energy' heaven of my embrace, everyone has unique pattern of energy and deserves to find their unique taste, and appreciate others.

A joyful, and caring home will truly become a home when it has taken into consideration all the people in it, and those who will come into it in the future. Hence it's important to see what will be my stable situation in the next 5 years and act like it. Remember if it wasn't perfect never to blame anyone for it, think of all the positive blessings you have had and move on gently to bring in more quality peace and harmony in your home. Life keeps upgrading and evolving so do our choices, and so do our home choices.

It's so important to give a voice to your likes and dislikes, and be someone whom it is a joy to live with, to be together with and a loving privilege to be with.

To maintain any space requires your joy, and also gentle detachment job of yours also remembering not to pollute or dirty the world, and to keep our spaces happy keeping and maintaining oru spaces happy, is only our responsibility.

Where does love live?

Keep this in mind as you clear your home, and consciously being aware of your attachments.

What is a sacred space?

A sacred space is a place with spiritual energy, this place is your altar your return to paradise, your place to pray or meditate or retreat.

A warm welcome

I welcome others into my home, here is the room I am most proud of, the kitchen crossroads of friendship and the worlds blessings- modern quote.

If there is harmony in the nation there will be harmony in the house, or country or city. If there is disharmony in the nation the houses will be naturally shaken lets take an example of a major catastrophy, or tsunami, or something that happens in the city that shakes us up.

I try to maintain my balance and peace no matter what Is happening so I can choose a response which magnifies my strength in my humanity to face the situation.

Angel virtues

Bring to mind the virtue of an angel. Then visualize the object or symbol to represent each virtue. For example a feather of lightness, a gift box for generosity a gratitude box for gratitude, and place them in your home.

The gratitude or peace table

One can practise this meditation before a family gathering to bring in goodwill to the occasion, visualize the dining table of your family members seated around it. mentally go around the table with your family members seated around it. and go around to each person sititng at the table, is there any tension between you too? Is there harmony or disharmony? Is there equality or inequality? And as you can begin to gather and understand your role better, your communication with the person will improve, This is the beauty of the Gratitude friendship and peace table.

Pictures of baby orangutans, Cheetahs, elephants and other small baby animals is said to be very nice to have in a family home too.

The present, and this moment

Painting by Neha Sharma, Jaipur

A humorous perspective on modern life.
Chicken feet means being pulled into every
distraction,
and getting excited about every thing
that comes,
and losing your peace and grounding
very easily'
Pregnancy gives you a chance to see situations
from a more calmer and gentler perspective,
More grounded and more peaceful,

More richer for the moment
Imagine your feet has the design of peace and
rest all over it,
Just like goddess lakshmis Lotus
Imagine you have feet like goddess Lakshmi
or Saraswati

We are technically given only two hands two
feet two legs,
Hence to try and do four tasks at once might
Decrease the quality of doing it
Mindfully so it is essential to do
One task at A time.
Without putting stress or pressure on
your doing,
But gentle awareness.

No routine is perfect if it is nourishing for you it is good enough right?

Why is my self time important?

Well you can ask yourself are you ignoring other areas of life which need your attention?

Self-time can also be a little silence time you can find during the day, the beautiful silence is meant to be respected and revered I used to be a little scared of silence as well but with time, as I've begun to enjoy my own company, and was lucky enough to learn yoga and meditation, silent time feels fresh all the time, and makes you feel truly loved by life in spite of what's going on.

And we also learn to enjoy the company of others with more quality.

I really have started revering and respecting my silent time, even if it's for two minutes per day. It can really connect me to my roots, guide me to make them more nourished, and wings feel more secure and gentle. And alert and aware.In olden times we didn't need too much self time because we got it automatically during sleep and few hours spent in our family temples, but today Lonliness makes one too secretive and a dangerous disease as it does not have any back up and the consequence is more of it.

Keeping a little time for silence in the day is a choice we make and reduces our stress levels. Just remember not to put that as an escape to fulfill your practical concerns.

Self time means going behind the scenes, than trying to be in spotlight all the time over caring parents will want to check on you to make sure you are fine constantly, you need to remind them, that your self time is important sometime and try to scrape out some self time for yourself, to go behind the scenes and notice what is happening, to make it more enriched and healthful and happy results you need self time. It is an investment of good sound health in your bank of surviving and thriving.

How it benefits the mind and body and spirit?

how one recreates their free time is your style and your creativity. Find out what suits you the best and refresh yourself?

Good graceful helpful silent time does
this to you
You regain a better perspective on a perceived
problem or off
You communicate more sensitively next time
you meet your partner.
You find a sense of natural flow of wellbeing
You feel refreshed and cleaerer
You feel centered and connected.

Not so good silent time

Can make you upset
And lonely and angry
Can make you feel uncomfortable.

In motherhood it is natural to wake up so many times of the night to feed the baby, that is why even 2-3 hours are not good enough for sleep sometimes, but then we have afternoon naps which allow the mother to nap during the day. We all find ways to cope in the best way possible if we are proactive, and involved in situations often however we might get attached to how situations should be, and how they should not have been and this causes us damage to live spontaneously and notice what Is happening.

It happens to everyone, does it happen to you also?

In times of overwhelment, When we feel we cant cope ask oneself three questions take 3 deep breaths.

Inhale- What Is happening around me?

Exhale- just 5 breaths

Inhale- What just happened?

Exhale just 4 breaths

Inhale What else could have happened (extended unnecessary response to a situation)

Exhale just 3 breaths

Inhale- Am I imagining into a future that is too far, to escape the present Moment?

Exhale

This will bring you in the moment and maybe show you a solution to a difficult situation.

We all are exposed to difficult situations, and in that case we must re call I intend to be ' peace under pressure' I choose to relax and find a better way to cope under pressure.

Flight or fight response- Flight or flight response in psychology means that is how usually animals are used to reacting because of survival responses they are learning to react and respond accordingly. We go back to the reptilian brain, It controls the basic heartrate, Breathing, body temprature and it is one aspect of our triune brain it is also called the primitive brain which is reactive because it wants to protect from harm and survive, it is written in modern psychology that we are social animals. Well what if we became social human beings, rather than just animals. True change is felt during pregnancy when we experience moments of compassion, truth, love, honesty, grace, joy and care. This opens the part of our brain or heart that is beyond flight or fight response, naturally. It is a big gift and meditation and good silent time and bring you in that space naturally.

I let go of the belief that we are social animals but we are Spiritual social beings having a human experience.

Fliht or fight response occurs when

When we are busy walking on the city streets gearing up for a rock music performance eating non veg.

In a wrestling competition trying to get attention when one is in this mode one is reacting automatically, sometimes it is necessary to push through and get tasks done, but if it is done out of intention to harm life it is not, when it is done out of intention to do things quickly it is mainly because it teaches us to be involved more in the task or work we are Doing and that is called Mindfullness.

So if one has a hurried up life, learning to relax and find few minutes to calm down breathe deep maybe even do yoga and be in nature and relax, this will benefit your balance enormously.

During pregnancy most women will try to find this gentle response and it is vital they must do so, Because this will help them feel at ease, so it is recommended you only watch ' flight or fight programmes only if you can handle it, just don't over watch because it can get brain to handle extra 'stimuli' and information.

Being affectionate with a loved one doing something that brings us joy looking at the stars moon or being in natural light.

These are excellent examples of flight to fight, and which means that, we are alert and we are ready to fight or flight away from what is happening, if it is too stressfull to face we will flight, otherwise one fights with the way it is but it will be the way it is, unless there is some change.

In stress full situations this brain gets activated, imagine being in a peaceful cozy home and bringing in the energy of the roads inside the home, or the metro, it is heavy and stressfull only for you, and not for the other occupants, because a cozy warms energy is more peaceful while at home, than the rushing energy of the world.

Now imagine eating a very heavy meal on your Bed. Your brain will want to relax but you are bringing in a heavy meal on your bed which will go against the restful response your body might wants to experience.

When you get stressed about a situation try to see it from a building which is 8 storey high above and look below, and imagine how someone is looking at you facing a stuck situation, this is one Beautiful way to come out of it. I call this ' the gentle understanding view or perspective.

But in the Mindfull way we can begin to, asking ourselves realise and do.

We cant tottally shut out, the world, its impossible, but we can seek a better response to stresfull situations.

1. **What happened**

2. **What is happening?**

3. **And am I imagining extra?**

Reflection moments...

What is purity?

- Pure
- Understanding
- Reverence.
- In
- Truth
- Yours.

How do I understand the nature of my desires and thoughts that I meet when I spend time alone/ or with myself.

Below are some reflections I realized I can depend on in my alone time and carving out what I truly want.

If you have a pure thought, nurture and nourish that more over Thoughts of hatred, attention, which feels good for a while but does not have a strong foundation. If you want to get stable but you have 100 other unstable thoughts they are coming up to actually give more fuel to the one Pure thought. Everything helps us to achieve our dreams when it is taken in the right time, manner understanding truth and purity.

For example

I want to do this and I want to do that, and I want to do it all.... calm down focusing on one good quality goal at a time is much better than so many thoughts at once.... (something will seem out of balance)

Pregnancy is a time to surrender more and reflect on what matters and prepare a beautiful environment for the coming child, Every child that is born again is a sign that unconditional love is not lost.

The oxygen of love and more on making positive space for your baby inner and outer.

Love and compassion are pure emotions that flow naturally between our hearts if we allow it.

Love is so much like the oxygen of the mind body And spirit. It allows us to be breathe and feel blessed and it purifies energizes and uplifts all it touches. You can reflect on in your alone time.

- Love
- Friendship
- Celebration
- Gentleness
- togetherness
- creator

- Beauty
- Peace
- Care

Relations hips (in relations we connect hip to hip with another literally) im talking about intimate ones, are you taking care of your hip? Hip is your hip, your lower part your seat, one has to take care of the Hip in relationships, the foundation and then the qualities can bloom within and with it. The last thing we reflect on our pregnancy is

- Strategy
- Work
- Competition
- Business
- Stress
- In our pregnancy

In fact all this can cause miscarriage and stress in pregnancy.

loving traditions called hooponopono is a loving prayer which says please forgive me, I m so sorry I love you and thank you.

Do you know Hooponopono was created by Morrnah Simeona in Germany, and there is a training for this course too?

This means that we say these four statements before an important event or even before sleeping, as sleeping with a heavy heart or mind does lead to nightmares and even attracting toxicity during sleep, because when we are asleep we are passive we are suspectible to the tension in the environment, toxicity and else, to deal with this say this prayer imagine it reminding you of your beautiful strength and then cover yourself with the prayers power and sleep. What steals the sensitive gentle movement.

- Reckless texting.
- Too much technology.
- Too much thinking
- And eating fast foods
- No exercise

And complaining to the moment. This stops the graceful flow of exchange we can benefit from a positive environment and what our mother earth so beautifully nourishes us with. And also watch your sensory Diet if you aren't happy with that, change it now.

Sensory diet means the information you are taking in through your five senses which is telling your brain about, the environment the world and yourself, and also watch the sensory diet your children will imbibe will be much like what you had, also watch your mental diet and emotional diet, are you taking in more than you can handle? If yes and no find positive ways to change, heal and get organized before you have your pregnancy which will need your purity commitment to make gentle and positive space for baby.

Spending time in the night sky and the morning sun have nourishing benefits beyond measure and can give us positive sleep and even more energy during the day. In the olden times it was natural to live in harmony with these cycles, we should never forget the loving moon and the nourishing golden sun rays power to heal and nourish our cells body and mind. Obviously in winters its natural to cocoon back into oneself, but the sun is even more nourishing to be around in winter. Don't allow other peoples allergies, moods, desires and habits stop you from your nourishing routine which will bring greater health and fulfillment during your pregnancy.

I remember the rhythm and movement of the larger cosmos and depend on It for my nourishment.

Its so important to find harmony with your own tastes likes and dislikes. Having strong likes or dislikes toward anyone or events means that you are getting judge mental about someone or something without your gentle reasoning power. Its so important to find your likes and dislikes, and also be flexible and patient with others especially if you are above 40. You must know very clearly what you like or dislike more clearly.

I am gentle with my baby's developing likes and dis likes as they grow up, and write in their toddler dairy and give it to them when they grow up, about how I saw them growing up from my eyes.

What I see through my eyes, no one else can see the way I do that is why my being active healthy and motivated as a mother is important and essential, and even as a father or a parent.

The who will do WHAT list

As a homemaker and a new parent you will meet many tasks starting from smaller to bigger to difficult tasks, you cant be good at everything individually so pretending is foolish, and do what you are good at and are naturally good At. If you try to maintain a vehicle and have to take care of the baby imagine, the amount of work youll have to do, so let someone else maintain your Vehicle, and you do what you can do.

- I can do this
- I'm good at this.

I find this very difficult to do(I am not allowing the help there is for me) there can be someone else in the family who is better at that particular task than you.

We are all nieghbours, some close some far, some very near but we all live on Earth. So lets try to be happy, cooperative and kind to each other Always.

Mama	Papa	Grandparents	helpers	Other children
Wash laundry	Ironing	Grocery shopping	Wash dishes	Vacuum
	Dry cleaning drop off			Dust
Fold laundry		Prepare meals	Load dishwasher	Make bed
Put away laundry	Dry cleaning pick up	Lunch	General home care	
		Dinner		
			Clean bathrooms	
		breakfast		

Mama	Papa	Grandparents	helpers	Other children
Water plants Take out trash	Feed pet Clean up after pet Walk the dog Yard work	Get the mail Pay the bills Banking	Vehicle maintainence	Feed baby
Diaper changes	Bathe the baby	Get the baby at night for feeding	Bathe the baby	Comfort the baby.
Care for other children	Manage guests	Comfort baby in fussy times.		

Notice which tasks from above you can do, and you cant do, and also notice which ones your husband or another family member does much gracefully than you, and then you can gently allow yourself to become good at what you can do.

As you read above, being a homemaker requires effort and energy, but it also depends on whether you are the cause of stress or liability or you are a cause of ease sensibility and faith..

Treating childhood Minor Illnesses

Fever: Crush garlic and put on feet And put socks on this recipe cures fever.

Cold: Ginger honey with banana.

Insomnia: One spoon of turmeric in warm milk with honey.

Sore throat: Water and salt

Vomiting: Clove oil application on the throat and nasal area and rest.

Ear pain : Visit to a Paediatrician

Cough: Check their diet. Or quality of water they are drinking Add cardamom in their diet.

No one can explain how gracefully and effortlessly are nose, hands, skin is formed in the womb, it is the nature's intelligence at work at the most divine level'

Happy senses, loving senses

Allergies are very common, for this make sure they are exposure to something that was incompatible to the body from the enviorment, the brain is learning to identify the different smells.

For senses to function beautifully we don't need to them to be overused, We need them to be happy. And god has made much more in the world to keep us happy. Its just about the focus. You also have to teach the child to remain warm, and protect themselves from harm. Consious healthy and positive exposure is the key always, (anything dangerous at an impressionable age). Smart exposure is the key to bring up mentally, emotionally healthy children. Start with yourself try Try altering your behaviours. That attract difficulties and complications and be kind not over sensitive.

Teaching yourself and your child this gentle prayer, thank you nature, for curing me holistically naturally and nurturingly.

That put me back in happiness and remind me of my body's gentle abilities to renew and heal.

Dangerous diseases

- Chicken Guneia
- Typhoid
- Jaundice
- Chicken pox
- Diahrea

Can be treated with good nutrition rest and doctors prescribed medicines.

We all want children who never get ill, well everyone gets ill atleast few times in their lifetime, we all try to find a way to heal, sometimes healing takes time and sometimes there is a quick recovery. When someone is ill we want him to recover quickly right, then we have to check in the quality of air/ water they are exposed to daily, and also the materials and interactions they have with toys, and the natural world. All illnessess happen due to exposure to something the body wasn't compatible or agree with whether it is toxin, or a habit.

No one lives a total pure lifestyle, we dispose off so much trash in the environment daily and we mistreat and contribute to the air pollution and water pollution. You must make sure your children are getting enough O2 every day.

Exercise get fresh air. Consume essential fatty acids.

Breathe properly avoid too much drugs or alcohol. Make food in healthy cooking oils. Avoid too much salt and keep all tastes in moderation.

Gentle writer believes

A healthy and positive world view invites in
more in harmony than conflict
And offers us a chance to lovingly take
responsibility
For our perceptions and where we come from.
Conflicts can be discussed privately,
Never to berete another's view point but to
Find atleast one commonality or agreement
Never to attract attention or fake Admiration

There is always scope for improvement.

Hosting worries & regrets

Regrets are little emotions and thoughts that we push aside because they are painful to see watch and go into and face but until we don't face them or understand them how will we grow realisation there?, regrets will take away the space of the growing and healthy realization of a truthful harmonious and happy life, when we have those little realizations, we can let go of regrets and embrace our realizations. This makes us want to value life even more.

I life my life regret free.
I let go of all my regrets.

Life is fresh and deserves my best now.
Living life regret free is the most beautiful goal
I do everything good now and that's what
really matters.

We usually take our regrets into the space where we avoid ignore life, what is happening around us now and what structure and solidity we need to rely on now rather than dwelling in liquid imaginings which have no substance anymore, don't dwell in regrets, stay near your realization.

Painful emotions can house inside our being if we don't give more space to those emotions which actually deserve the beautiful space within and around us. So don't regret anything, treat those emotions like guests and the other emotions as first priority because its not worth it to give house to what drains you, rather than what sustains you fully.

'How refreshing it is to hear the whinny
packhorse
when its burden is lifted off its back'

Exposure- life is full of risks, the risk of meeting, the risk of giving, the risk of loving, we must throw ourselves into these risks with all our hearts, count your blessings.

Counting our blessings gives house to them than house to regrets fear or apprehension!

Life counts

'In the end it is not the years in your life that
count it is
the life and love in your years'

To be a helpful adjuster

Don't fix plans to how your baby will adjust, keep babys environment calm and quiet, try wrapping him snuggly to minimize extra stimulation and stress. Hold him gently and avoid the extra bouncing, jiggling or excessive patting. And demonstrate happiness to him in the best capacity you can, and you help him Be involved with life and all the be, Do's and Have.

The weather does not adjust to us we adjust to the weather, the city does not adjust to us, we adjust to the city, same goes with seasons, so it makes sense to find more gratitude the day does not adjust to us, we adjust to the day, same way the baby has to learn to be an adjuster, he or she will cry will feel uneasy, but that's what babies Do, the Keep the room refreshed, keep it clean and spacious.

Offer life our best, keep it simple clean and minimal. On the go (which room to use for what) and don't get attached to any room. (understand and take responsibility for your energy).

When a room quietly invites in the the loving calmness of the moon and the morning sun, it shines bright needing Just little space and brings in relaxation and calmness.In the olden times we needed a room to be sheltered, stay protected find calmness And find our comfort zone, and anything in excess leads to imbalance, Now we use room for many purposes, including letting out our fears thoughts problems about the world, remember never to dump in all your problems in a space, just because someone is offering you a good space the way you use it defines you. but if you feel afraid about anything discuss in an environment where you feel safe, relaxed in faith and loved and cared for.

A sleep room should be for sleep and rejuvenating ideally. A prayer room for praying. A classroom is for studying and learning. A kitchen room for cooking. A bathroom for having a shower. A drawing room for drawing agreements, or sharing. A bar room for drinking and a baby area for napping, caring and keeping the baby from any kind of harm.

Notice which energies room you ignore in your world, that is where you are imabalanced socially and it is temporary.

For example I hardly find time to find joy in family life and find pleasure in get togethers- *drawing room energy*.

I hardly find time for relaxation and solitude- prayer room energy. I don't find sleep refreshing- *bed room energy*.

Hence you can try to identify which rooms energy you need in you life for example you need more sleep and quiet time in your bedroom so simply avoid doing any activities that would energise or produce a lot of stimulation, and keep it for the study area or a classroom. Don't make your room the all in all, using it for its purpose invites more stability and clarity in ones being and life.

For example if you bring in all your sorrows of the day and your unfulfilled expectations to your bed you will overwhelm yourself, god only helps those who can help themselves.

The sacred Trinity
- Mind
- Body

- Spirit
- Harmony Or disharmony.

We experience both in daily life, and situations can break our a self esteem if we are in denial of where our mind wants to focus, and where i want to lead the focus what my body wants to do in the coming weeks, and what i am imposing it should do.

What my heart feels like doing spontaneously And I am putting harsh rules rituals or philosophies to it, this spoils the trinity, and can make one feel imbalanced and out of place It happens with everyone, its possible to feel in trinity when we take good care of our mind body and soul in the way it wants. And that takes little commitment focusing of attention and guiding your mind than letting it control or guide you. I feel out of place, it is exactly because of the trinity is out of flow of wellbeing and joy.

Homemaker affirmation: *I am honest, caring and loving about being a homemaker and it's a joy to share responsibilities and to get tasks done gracefully.*

Its safe to delegate and trust others, and never try to take all the burden on my shoulders alone.

Some invigorating and nurturing activities to try.

- Watch a romantic movie in the afternoon
- Let someone pamper your feet.
- Read some great children books
- Re-read the book you read when you were 9

- Read a biography of someone you admire.
- Have a gratitude party
- Pray for the world, or city or a problem in the world
- Stop looking backward and longing, start looking forward with anticipation.
- Put a do not disturb sign on your bedroom door.
- Learn a craft you've always wanted.
- Paint your bathroom one wall the color of the sea.
- Watch videos on television ou saw as a kid.
- Write in a gratitude journal, or talk to a friend about what you are in gratitude for.
- Make yourself a glass of chocolate milk.
- Learn chocolate making with. your lover.
- Be kind together and to someone unconditionally.
- Sit on a mountainside and watch the sunset.
- Have someone bring you your favorite breakfast.
- Go on a spa date.
- Give yourself a break.
- Wrap yourself in a super soft cashmere shawl.
- Stargaze twogether
- See through a telescope.
- Read poetry
- Swim out to the shore and see how small your problems are.
- Start a wish folder or a wish list
- Fill your day with meaningful activities
- Plant a specific flower.

- Dress in lush fabrics silk velvet and lace.
- Give fruits or vegetables to a Beggaron the street or the needy.
- Have a scalp massage.
- Respect the purity of life.
- Respect service.
- Be of service to someone
- Let your partner buy you a present you weren't expecting or were.
- Buy a present for your partner.
- Pray for someone some cause or just out of humbleness
- Join or pray together.(its v powerful)
- Surprise your parents with a gift.
- Use a bamboo toothbrush(good for the environment)
- Help someone in their suffering. Give share.
- A together activity.

What were some fun activities which will soothe you? you can ask other mothers in your community get together and do a fun and fulfilling activity.

Which plants can improve the air in my home?

Money plant- they improve your cognitive ability and make you smarter.

Care- you do not need water to them everyday. Money plants like water in big gulps so let the soil dry first. When you are watering it, make sure to do it thoroughly until water comes out of the drainage holes. Light it bight to semi dark light but no direct sun.

Soil- do not use regular garden soil because it contains impurities.

Fertilizer- If grown in a potting mix, feed your money plants every two weeks, in spring and summer with a balanced liquid fertilizer diluted by half. A balanced fertilizer will usually have the best way to incorporate this plant into your life. It is definitely your lungs best friend. Its also the most available plant in India.

Mother in laws tounge- This south African beauty in must have in ones home. The name is fitting because it is really difficult to kill this plant (which would mean, it should be good to listen to her intently with love and friendliness and compassion). These plants absorb harmful toxins like Nitrogen Oxide, Carbon monoxide from the air.

Care- its important to keep the soil a little moist in the growing season. In winter make sure the water is just enough to percent the soil from getting too dry.

Light- Ideally these plants require bright indirect light.

Bamboo plant

Bamboo plant are easily available all over the country and are one of the best things you can have around the house to arrest bad air. They are happiest when in the open, so if you have a large terrace. That would be the perfect place for your bamboo palm.

They can be kept indoors, especially because bamboo palms are adopt at lessening the Furniture they remove Formalydehyde purifier in and around your home.

Care- bamboo palms like bright, indoor light and prefer to remain moist, but too moist, Alternatively these plants can also be grown in water.

Light- they thrive in almost any kind of light, except direct sunlight, which starts turning yellow.

Soil- bamboo palms can be grown in water, change the water once a week, for a healthy plant and to avoid mosquito breeding. If grown in soil, it should be kept moderately moist.

Fertilizer- do not need soil or fertilizer to grow but it does need a good organic compost or Manure.

Do Try

Technology fast

We cant get off our phones, or computers we miss out so much of life, the song for birds, to the little things of life, sometimes we even miss out on the pleasant real flower, instead we are in the image of it, in technology fast our senses become cleaner and purer.

Too much TV or technology can make you feel tired, because we are exposing it too much radiation, and sometimes even programs that don't uplift us, imagine you are letting yourself get swayed with entertainment when you can control, controlling what to see and hear is wisdom.

Infrared saunas

Traditional environment uses a hot environment to promote sweating, they do little to heat up the external environment but work with infrared radiation to heat up your body internally. They can help raise your metalbolism and promote sweating in a safe way.

Through sweating you can release toxins, and infrared sauna brings out toxins just like Epsom salts.

What is epsom salts?

Using epsom salts and contacting floors and walls we built up chemicals from those substances, what Epsom salt does is, it can heal the toxins naturally just dip your towel in Epsom salt mixture and put it on your forehead or where ever there collects build up tension, it relaxes the skin immensely.

Non toxic infrared insect repellent

For insect repellent you can add, 10 drops of lavender oil, 10 drops of peppermint oil, 5 drops of geranium

Fill the mixture with water and spray it around your environment to keep insects away. It even gives of a pleasant healing fragrance.

Some fabric options for babies

Did you know?

To keep a watch for the below. When planning a Childrens Room it should be next to the master bedroom in the south.

Padded head board is preferable if while sleeping the child bangs his head it will be a problem. All furniture should have round edges. A bin to keep toys. Bathroom should be skid proof.

How to get rid of lizards

Pepper Pestiside spray: Make a pesticide spray by adding pepper and water Spray it in places like tube light corners under the fridge and under the stove.

Peacock feathers: Peacock feathers usually scare lizards.

Nepthaline balls: when you place Nepthaline balls under the stove, to water sinks and wardrobes., is a good pest control remedy. It not only acts against lizards but is very effective against cockroaches. Lizard repellents also called as Lakshman rekha, create some awkward noise which prevents the lizards from entering into the home.

How to keep away flies

Clear away all liquids clean food debris from under kitchen supplies. Make sure all rubbish bins have tightly sealed lids. Have drains and pipes cleaned to prevent fruit fly infections.

How to keep away mosquitoes

Use mosquito repellent on exposed skin. Use mosquito repellent candles.

How to prevent rats from entering your home

Check your metal containers and regularly clean under cookers and fridges. Rats come in through broken pipes make sure all pipes are closed. And well maintained sprinkle whole black pepper also keeps the rat away.

Try to keep away these items inches away from you

- Lighters
- Box cutters
- Axe
- Utility knives
- Guns
- Screwdrivers
- Martial art weapons
- Black jacks.
- Bleaching powder
- Wet cell batteries
- Laptops too close

They should be allowed near you by any means, in a public environment you cant avoid so avoid going to such places, and dwell in places which don't have all these devices in abundance. Clear them from near you for sure.

An empress should be around fruits, freshness safety and softness in all forms. You will read about what an emrpess is in Chapter three. Embracing the empress in you.

Home access and redefining changes in a home for safe home access for mother and baby

Its so important to keep in mind, the kind of furniture that has to be around the mother and baby because, anything that does not suit the baby's body will be difficult for the baby to reach, and hence there could be blunders or accidents. To avoid that please follow up the beneath changes.

Level walkways with no crack, holes, or gaps. Raised thresholds. Easily manage able door knobs and locks non-slippery outdoor steps. Secure hand railings. Well-lit entrance. Dry floor surfaces. Loose rugs and crimp edges. No cluttered magazines and toys on floor. No cords and wires on the floor. Stairs should not be in poor repair. No uneven steps. Clear access to bathroom, bedroom and kitchen areas.

Furniture to avoid:

Low lying furniture that obstructs your way. Cabinet shelves too high or too low. Beds too high or too low. Unstable chairs, sharp objects lying around should be kept in a toolbox.

Bathroom

Install grab bars in bathroom or shower. Install grab bars in the toilet. Low toilet seats Prefer non-slippery mats by the bathroom sink, preferably jute, those which don't allow slipping.

Stairway

Secure hand railings. Carpets or runners fastened down. Adequate lightning.

Lighting

Night lights in bedroom, stairway, hallways and living areas. Flashlight by your bed, only if necessary. Windows to let the lightening in. Other things to avoid: Loose or ill-fitting shoes, inappropriate, or ill measured walking aids and equipment. No designated area for pets. Wheelchair with dysfunctional brakes.

This is one of the most important elements you can add to your a home and for the sake of your long term health. Gardening is relaxing and meditative as well and also connects you with nature.

Be sure to choose organic seeds and they should be non genetically modified seeds. This will help you grow your organic garden easily and beautifully.

Ingredients for your garden

Fertilizer, A shovel, A ruler or measuring tape, Fencing supplies, Get your soil ready! *"To make a garden is to believe in a tomorrow." "Gardening is an art, that uses, flowers and plants as paint, and soil and sky as the canvas."*

**Plant smiles, grow laughter, and harvest love;
He who plants a garden, plants happiness.**

What to grow, all year around!?

Every month has its own vegetables which grow the most during each month, hence the chart below defines what to 'grow' all year around, it can be helpful while trying to grow our home grown vegetables and fruits, and henceforth have a beautiful garden of your own. Check in the table below what grows mostly in each month enjoy.

Its very safe to garden during pregnancy. But in limits you can have fresh grown food. To enhance health of your family. It's a time saver and its theraputic.

Message to the reader

Why I call this chapter Neighbours of the heart is because we all have lots of nieghbours everyday, the ones sitting next to us while we travel the ones whom we share some time with the ones we share a lot of time with but eventually we know who the Nieghbour of our heart is because they are our true heart keeper And hold the most closest space for us(space keeper) whom do you give that privilege to? is your giving. (the ones closer to heart) This chapter was easy to write since I have a degree in Feng Shui and had good knowledge of homes I pay credit to this amazing book called the Book of balance in which there is some excellent information regarding what kind of furniture environment a baby should be brought up in from railings to floors this chapter also hosted some self soothing techniques which were meant to be in the Empress chapter but I had put it here because ,but the awareness of not bringing negativity at our homes from outside is very important it keeps a space holy and loving. This chapter had to be very factual also It gradually formed in my mind after noticing something positive about my home a lot of money goes into building a home maintaining it and its important to make our children aware of that since we all tend to take the home energy for granted sometimes being reckless or careless in this department is not a sign of a practical caretaker! Well our homes are a temporary abode while we are here on this planet but they should not be less nourishing kind value based and adhere to the individuals heart felt needs.

Reflection: We all have been drifters dreamers once in a while but when we begin to settle that is when our tastes Likes and dislikes become more refined' and closer to who we really are.

- Are you a joy to live with? Its safe to create a firm foundation for a joyful life'

- Notice 5 things about your current home that you really like.

- In the last week or 20 days, or even 3 days, who helped you the most with an important chore?Why was the chore important?

- Quote to ponder

- Build on the beauty of your truth, than depend on loftiness or impermanence of lies.

Notes

1. What were some of the favourite lines from this chapter. How did it make you Feel?

_____

_____

_____

_____

_____

_____

_____

_____

_____

2. What insights did you receive to make your experience more enriching and meaningful?

_____

_____

_____

_____

_____

_____

_____

_____

_____

Caring Chapter 3

Embracing caring and enriching
family and essential support
Marriage of Heart Mind and Soul

DON'T WORRY
BE HAPPY

MEHER BABA

Throughout the previous chapter you read how to make an ideal home space for the baby and mother reveling over some poems written by me and readings on how to make a sacred space now its time to walk into creating gratitude safety and beauty, nurturing and protecting our family life.

With the most intimate part of our lives our family. Well, we do realize that its so important to honor each member of the family equally, equality respect love and care invites happiness and joy within the members of the family in the kindest ways, Well it truly is so healthy for an infant to have a healthy and witness a loving caring diversely connected social community, In this chapter you will explore and read on everything that makes a family special and more close and bonding.

Enjoy the beautiful exploration of the *cells and viens of our lives*. This chapter is bountiful with bubbling joy because I have shared how important is a loving social group connection, and valuing each other's differences to keep marriage conflicts at ease and how important it is to make proper efforts in this area of life. Your diverse social group affects the baby that will come in the world wont it? As well so make the right efforts to create a social environment that suits you and your needs, and provides you and your infant a possibility of a happy healthy enriched life.

Pray.
Peaceful ray of yours.

* voice of love*, voice of togetherness
If you ever heard the true voice you recall
and Realize that Love wins over lust.
And gratitude wins over guilt
Forgiveness wins over fear
Peace wins over possession

Every place be filled with welcoming and joy
May there be lesser violence,
And the sun shines with insight in every sky,
And everyone be given their right,
To exist beautifully and gracefully.
Sweet wish.
We all have dreamt, of a world that is joyful,
And we all contribute to it with
following our joy.

Or at least will make it possible....slowly
but surely..

Pray for the kind of society you want to live in
and be that quality everyday.

These are amazing wins because if love wins over lust we wont ever fall just for lust, If gratitude wins over guilt we will not allow guilt to win no matter what We take responsibility if forgiveness wins over fear, we will never not fear living with dignity grace an purity. If peace wins over possession, we wont allow such acts to happen in our culture and country. If healing wins over hurt we wont allow ourselves to stay hurt for very long either.

What prayers come within your heart?

Intention- to let go of dominating a conversation, but inviting equality love and feeling of honest communication.

The mother and baby are connected so closely, that the baby will react to, and through the mother's discomfort and feeling about something' it is truly a bond that is divine'

I love this song which truly brings peace of mind and heart.

Grant me peace of heart,
Before others and things I don't understand,

I want to think of what I do understand and
follow that.
Give me peace of heart.

Conficts and negativity
Be removed from my heart
If others make mistakes,
Keep me away from lies,
I want to give power to love and truth.

When difficulties arise,
Have some mercy on me,
I intent to keep my hope and faith,
Before worshipping any one,
Id worship my truth and intuition.

Grant me peace of heart and mind.

Humko man ki shakti dena, man vijay karien
Duskro ki jai se pehele khudko jai kare
(intuition)
Humko man ki shakti dena
Doosro ki jai se pehele, khud kojai karien

Bhed bhaav,
Apne dil se, saaf kar sake
Doston se bhool ho to, maaf kar sakien.
Jhoot se bache rahien, sach ka dum bharien.

Mushkalien pare to hum pe itna karm kar,
Saath dene to dharm ka, chalien to
dharm par,

Khudh pe hausla rahien badi se na dare,
Doosro ki jai se pehele,
Aapko jai karien (intuition,)

Humko man ki shakti Dena
Man Vijay karien.

I remember this was my school prayer
which we used
To sing in our school assembly meeting, i
Always sang but truly understood the meaning
of it today and it is beautiful.

Whenever you understand your truth is
the right time for you.
Individually.

Value and appreciate

Even if you feel no one values or appreciates you don't worry every ones felt the way sometime, Valuing ourselves and appreciating ourselves and seeing the best in ourselves and others attracts grace love and cooperation, The beauty of appreciation is that it takes us to where we truly feel belonged happy and wanted.

I once carried an orange in my bag on the way out, and saw these little children on the foot path sleeping on a dirty cloth blanket I realized and hoped the orange would make them happy and give them comfort, well there wasn't an orange tree there but they did deserve to sleep in a clean atmosphere and well fed. you can even give guavas an tomatoes.

There was also a thought in my mind to provide them with clothes or an extra blanket or hoped they would get work

Living an existence like that is so painful, and difficult it feels good to make it a little easy for someone else.

Togetherness

Time of Gratitude, enrichment, truth, honesty, enthusiasm, reverence. Nurturing, encouragement, soulful, surrender.

"Together is the most honest and real and kindest place to be"

When the seed starts going towards a destructive imbalanced state that is when we need to be concerned about ourselves and our children. Children become more destructive and secretive if not guided properly and left to their own devices, it makes them more complicated and feel separated. these days well mannered and grounded adults are a sign of a balanced happy normal childhood, with less exposure, to the digital world. How we have evolved since Carriage 600 Bc to airplane 1903, and also since the most important innovations like telephonic and mobile phones. Many people complain about the annoyingness of mobile phone ringing continuously but it is actually you who is allowing yourself to get impacted. You can either realise and use it minimum and quality or you can mis use it its all dependent on the individual, always.

Prayerful Family affirmations

Every day I thank God for a wonderful family.
Every person in my family is healthy
and happy.
I allow myself the freedom to be myself.
I am setting a great example for my children.
I am providing my children with a
brilliant future.
My family is supportive of my actions
and goals.

Nourishing your family soul

Family
Feel the love within you and give yourself an inner namaste.

Who is a mindful and heartfull parent?

A parent is like a Sunlight during pregnancy, and the child is the seed because the parents world view lightly impacts the child's world view, isnt it?

We all have seen positive and negative sides of parenting, and that is why it is essential to realize to thank them.

What do you love about your parents? Do you thank them for the pain they take to do small things for you, or you forget their little acts for you?

True parenting requires us to be flexible and never forceful, it requires us to surrender to trust and evolve in a more healthier and happier way.

A an intelligent and caring parent and child will make sure that affection and attention of parents is not taken for granted, and that no and in recognizing their child's unique talent or potential there is a lot of harmony care and interest in their becoming their of their most unique individual selves.

Parents are doing the best they are doing. Aren't they? So are we understanding or cooperating enough?

Parents are our biggest well wishers: they will give us the tools as we grow up to be and stay healthy guardians and protectors: they will do their best to keep us away from fire, which means senseless acts they will do their best to keep away from negative acts of societies, and keep us in a good healthy social circle as much as they can.

Caretakers and conflict resolution makers- you will notice a good parent will teach siblings equality and friendship and care, negative parenting will compare the children, parents aren't superhuman nor will you be, parenting is a skill and an art which we learn from each other and the society in general about what works and what does, when we find an approach, we can trust and reap the benefits of a approach that makes parenting an enriching process.

So what are some approaches?

Mindful parenting requires us to not compare the child with others and teach them to value their Unique selves. It means acknowledging their actions in the present, because past is history yet good to contemplate on positively and love is present. It means to not strive for perfection, but enjoying and being true to ourselves. It means making note that you consciously improving on your self esteem, helps the child work on theirs. Some children don't listen to their parents because they don't 'hear anything worthwhile to learn from them. Mindful parenting means, doing the best you are doing and knowing that that is enough. Being a mindful parent doesn't mean being dominating we had to use this tool, in the past so we were heard. Mindful parenting requires us to be appreciators, than discouragersx. It means to remember that they are playing the role with the best knowledge and faith they have in the moment. Its about teaching them to increase the size of their faith and decreasing the size of worry. Gentle parenting feels fresh heart-full understanding and full of nourishment care and Genuine connection and togetherness. Its to remember to nurture and guide a child's sensibilities and sensitivities.

I believe the children are our future, teach them well and let them lead the way, show them all the beauty they possess (hold) inside.

-from the song
Greatest love of all.

And to never stop 'believing in the beauty of
their 'dreams'
It means to teach them the difference between
right and wrong.

To be in your children's memories 'Tommorow'
you have to be in their lives 'today'
Mindful parenting means being willing to make
a gentle shift from fear to love.
And acknowledging the little efforts
of everyday
And smiling at the little victories everyday
And never forgetting to shower children
With
Affection, attention and acknowledgement as
Much you give yourself.

In all the world, you deserve your love and
affection the most
Words of 'Gautam buddha'

'There is no greater romance
In Life, than being receptive to your own truth
and realization'– Meher Baba.

Why do we work so much?

To sustain and keep our families happy and secure, the father is a breadwinner and the mother is the nurturer.

- Over-working.
- Just don't over work
- or work 'hard'.
- Working gently,
- Softly and happily!
- Doesn't that sound Better!

Isn't that enough?

Make it a point to watch when you are losing interest. It could mean your energy is being scattered / You are giving passively You aren't receiving with alertness and awareness. You cant relate clearly You aren't valuing your own energy.

Finding that and closing that gap, and keeping the interest fresh and alive is a skill gained with meditation and self awareness.

Everyday in every way I am renewing my interests and faith, boundaries are so important to keep in mind not the fence boundaries only but solid bark boundaries between one tree and another one tree does not climb on another trees space without its permission, nor does one plant climb over another's growth they grow where they grow even 1 or 2 inches apart happily. As an individual it is important to watch and guard your boundaries with the gentle care, this is not only a positive and nourishing habit toward yourself and others but it so important to and feels right in your body.

Same like that our relationships with each other, we need to respect another trees space / energy time in our life otherwise we lose our grounding and become spaced out in relating to other persons life!

Imagine you have roots going down and you are a tree, your branches are your thoughts, leaves are your memories, now let the ones which want to go fall, and the ones which want to stay stay in your awareness so does everyone have their own thoughts and roots now imagine when you try to over power another by putting force now that is really violating but we human beings are social people and intelligent and so is nature but we must learn positive healthy boundaries to feel and keep sane at all times!

Clear boundaries

Protecting and respecting your time, energy and sharing resources wisely

You feel violated, so to not let that happen, always put clear boundaries with others this is where you cant enter my personal space, and this is where I wont enter yours. In a world of social media and information, two vices are feeling scattered, abusing information or others energy.

Hence to protect your energy value the time you spend on social media. Every hour is your honorable time to share your time space energy, Many women who call themselves career women say that having a baby has been a turning point in their life, where it puts them back to what really matters as a woman. However, women aren't just reproductive machines our lives are meant to be holistic and inclusive of both work and play, and work that satisfies us. How to find that work? Just know that whenever you are doing some activity where the feeling of joy, and your creativity, is being applied nicely, and you aren't just getting praise, but you gain confidence, strength, and contribution, that's the best work that that feels fullfilling and nourishing to the heart.

But usually this is how it is, our true family makes us feel nourished and centered, happy and connected.

Your circle of love and belonging

Who is in it?

Poem written in 2016.

Just for today I wont condemn anyone
Just for today I wont criticize
Just for today I wont over expect.
Just for today I will let go of what I am not
under control.
Just for today I wont panic
Just for today I will take 10 deep breaths
before doing anything new.
Just for today, I will take responsibility and
change a wrong habit
Just for today I wont judge anyone
including myself.
Just for today I will allow myself to Be.
Just for today ill notice something
good someone

Just for today ill let go of anger
toward someone.
Just for today ill embrace the beauty of today.
Just for today ill forgive myself

Because my today
Creates my tomorrow.

Affirmation
I will find acceptance in today, and create
harmony for tomorrow.

The role of in-laws

The kind role of in-laws

My second parents. Till you arent in respect and care with your in-laws, the law of making them your parents isn't complete. Every new relationship which needs sunlight first needs strength of soil and effort. And togetherness feels as if it blissfull and beautiful and natural the relationship becomes sharing and joyful and kind how our differences meet, different lives, different backgrounds, cities different nieghbourhoods sometimes different countries!, we understand that we were meant to meet and just like how its meant to be, with support, creativity fun joy and growth. So it should be a loving law, to be in harmony and care with your in laws. I love and respect my inlaws and open myself to enjoy a harmonious connection together and truthful connection together.

Find out 6 qualities or more you can appreciate about your inlaws and the gifts you can give and receive from them.

1.

2.

3.

4.

5.

6.

7.

As I was writing this chapter beginning from Pray poem to value poem, I was doing a mind body spirit wholeness course, and as the words were flowing through me I realized this has to go in the family and essential support chapter, I remember the value of spiritual time in a day plus gratitude does truly make us feel deeper at peace and centered and grounded during the day, in a world of pointless distractions its essential and important, as you read the value poem, I actually had the experience of giving someone oranges, than eating them all by myself, and I also wished that there were orange trees planted on the streets! So everyone would get their share, well as you will go below you will now read one of the most deepening and interesting paragraph of the chapter, wisdom and weeds where I talk about the possibility of spiritual growth with our parents relationship, I felt this relationship together with the relationship we have with money and family does impact our growth and wellbeing, to have amazing enriching relationships here is what one can truly aim for, because at the end of the day we think about the most important people we share our life with, all the poems are written by me, in a thoughtful creative alert state, and I always said a gentle prayer before writing as it makes the writing positive, when we do anything important its so important to stay positive and happy. You will read paragraphs from role of husband, to a loving thank you to grand Parents. Reading this chapter with the eyes of your heart as you will feel your heart expanding to the love for your close ones, as I certainly did during writing and much more. Anytime we are insensitive to this area, all our areas suffer. Hence it is so important to build a relationship based on mutual trust care and friendship, whats growing? wisdom or weeds.

Children are not distraction from more important work, They are more important than work'(unless they are distracting you a lot and not understanding

In context of parenting, obstacles and facing life and each other, as we are.

> When a parent tells his children
> Im looking forward to what you choose
> How you grow
> How you learn and live
> How you turn out
> And I hope to watch you

And care and love you the same!

You can handle it
How we grow wisdom and recognise Weeds.

When you just pay attention to your actions deeds and what you are doing and contributing you don't bully another or make them like you, you can learn from them but you never make them like you. it crushes their individuality and beauty and growth.

When we explore together and with each other and for each other for the best rather than just self satisfaction or to be fixed we are growing wisdom.

When we stand for each others growth and integrity than fear each other we are growing wisdom. When we don't get threatened by each others growth we are truly giving attention and planting more wisdom, growing Weed Seperates us wisdom unites us back again. Wisdom brings fulfillment weeds bring grounding and not getting spaced out.

There was once a very chirpy bird knocking on the glass of the window I found it really cute and while I was writing this I got an insight, I felt the little bird is telling me to come out and play, don't be so serious and move so seriously on the journey of life, the little bird can come in the form our friends, our loved ones when we get too heavy and serious and start drowning and frowning at our growth and that point you need to start noticing whether it is feeling good to grow here or you feel stuck in the ways you follow....

I felt she said, come out and play, don't take it all too heavy life goes on eternally and its not worth it to lose balance because we are stuck in a way of being.

Wisdom is noticing these *gentle moments* of care which life gives us it is also not resisting the flow of wellbeing and enjoying life as It comes I would have regretted if I took it all very seriously and didn't enjoy these small moments and heeded them

Also a gentle balance of inside, outside is so important we become weed when we don't get social emotional And physical nourishment and we close ourselves to the wonder and beauty of life we all have these moments but I wont forget the cute bird knocking on my window while I was writing!

The son is always trying to be the provider, earnesingly that's his role in life, daughter is the receiver here but she has to value the effort to invite her brother to value her and protect her when he can, same goes for a husband.

Giving and receving nourishment from Life:-

Weeds- a plant that is not valued where it is growing, and is usually has vigorous growth, especially one that tends to overgrow or choke out more desirable plants Weeds are not needed, where your wisdom grows, but Weeds- still they grow, but you can, and remove them. And let the desire-able plants grow.

It is the same, with our true desires, either we give sunlight (the nourishments from our hearts, and respecting our and others capacity to give) and nourishment to them, and focus there, or we give sunlight and nourishment to weeds. And ignore the wisdom. A weed is also like a learning experience.

Wisdom: The quality, of having experience, knowledge, and good judgement the quality of being wise.

It's better to have lots of wisdom growing in your garden than weeds, that which wither and die, and are no good for the fertility, of and strength of the and soil and soul, we let the weed grow but only we have to remove it again from the garden.

I feel all meetings are meant to happen and are fated, people come into our lives for various reasons;, however, when we realize what is the reason, in our meditation, or in our spiritual side, we discover that everyone who comes into our lives, has a purpose, which is short lived or long lived, we just have to recall, to keep shining our best, and see who stays.

Because the one who decides to stay is going to help us grow more wisdom in the garden of our heart. And that also over for a long time this person deserves a very high and a good quality position in your life.

Do give it a chance give such and position to the special such people in your life. Not everyone deserves a high quality position in our life, well obviously we allways decide!

The son needs to remember that the daughter can also support herself in other ways so there is no race to be the best supporter or son, just to do the best one can do is good enough. Beliefs like my children wont take care of me when they grow up - attracts fear and worry(weed).

As we grow up and weighs us down. Wisdom is remembering and knowing that our children can be different than us and they will be but they also will have their own ways to grow and as more experienced we can guide them better but we don't own them!

Perfectionism is an illusion, love and wisdom is the truth

I've seen parents getting depleted and frustrated. It is natural to have frustrations and depletions, but we slowly and gently realize that being a loving parent takes daily nurturing and watering the seed of love, and keeping the emotions flowing. We cannot be the entire sunlight but we can have enough water and wisdom to bring them up. No one can be the entire sunlight for anyone, but we all have bits of sunlight from our big creator.

Instilling faith and friendship in divine keeps us confident about doing the best that we are doing, and that is good and sacred enough.

You're being the best parent or grandparent that you can be, Or great grand parent, just remember that we all share this time, it is a celeberation! Hence, cooperation is the key to realizing that sharing your love and hope and wisdom with each other our highest love and our deepest prayer.

The practice of Mietta of loving kindness focuses unconditional friendliness towards self and others, send mietta to yourself and others.

May you be happy, may we be happy

May you be secure, may we be secure
May you be wealthy, may we be wealthy.

Give Mietta often to yourself and others
This is sacred.

When a wife has a good husband it is easily shown on her face, and (likewise) even the husbands face- Goethe quote
The bonds of my life are my happy place during my pregnancy'

In Zibu, this symbol means 'eternal love and bond'

Role of husband (Husbond') and family support

Dear Husbond of your wife, your wife is going to go through these 9 months, and she will need your support. We understand that you aren't a nurse or a doctor (giggles) or if you are it's great. Well she will need your, love, care, availability shoulder time, gentleness, touch therapy, as much as you can give during this process. *(blushes)* I recommend, making her feel special. Get her gifts once in a while, make her the happiest you can, know what makes her happy know what makes you two happy.because a happy couple makes a happy Pregnancy and even Parenting.

She is going to go through backaches because of the extra weight, so make sure she isn't carrying anything super heavy, She will have a heavy bladder, she is carrying many more kilograms than what she's used to, so lighten her load by connecting with her with your care, remind her of how beautiful she is. It's very nourishing to know but do, try to make it worth it by taking her on a holiday after the third trimester. Please read this book with her as well. There are many recipes in the book that you can browse through and make what your wife likes.

Thank you in Gentleness and Care.

- How do you know he loves you?
- How do you know he cares?
- Does he take you out dancing just so he can hold you close?
- Dedicate a song just for you?

Hel find his way to you with the little acts of love and much more, That's how you know he's yours and the one. Little bit from the song That's how you know from the movie 'Enchanted'.

When it comes to men who are romantically involved with you its very simple. Paying equal attention to what they say is better than what they do same goes with women actually!

By the way the symptoms of inner peace are, loving yourself and others. Appreciation not judging another less worry more wisdom. Tendency to act based on hope than fear.

I think.. Love actually means having time to nurture a 'bond'. It's a Bond. as I have noticed, till now. It takes effort time and maybe even faith and every bond is unique and joyous.

Whenever anyone asked me, what kind of love are you creating, not finding, usually when we stop looking and finding it is there.

I said, "Well, the one that, you can depend 'with' and 'on' truly, that's called, lifetime waala love." (a love that can stand through storms, shivers, intruders, and bring in peace joy and harmony to it). Is worth investing in isn't it?

I realized to have an equal relationship we have to overcome and move above the ' I will stay single forever story' well yes many people decide to stay unmarried, *but if you want to get married* and recognize and seize the opportunity fully you must practice the above because living with yourself all these years you are only thinking about yourself, the people who are self consumed cannot have a healthy happy marriage. I had to let go of so many habits, to allow someone in like wanting the whole bed space for myself, and eating the way I want without considering what they like, sharing spaces closets, wallets, time and much more. I evolve from being self centered to thinking for others. Life experiences are much better when we care for others.

This is the longest and purest form of honeymoon we could ever take, we are both worthy of this bond and connection.

Your best vibes:

Give her gifts of Loving strength and care, Fresh air open windows, inside outside time balance, Nourishing sleep routine, Your friendship and faith, Hydration, Improving heath, Increased positive energy, Authority and protection, Laughter and love, Less stress, Massage, Organic foods, Deep listening- Listen with your whole being, Time to recover, Sobriety, Gentle stretching, Sunlight.

Children develop childlike qualities like awe love playfullfullness and innocence and joy when their mother is lovingly pampered.

Activity: Make a gratitude board or a list together, contemplate on a happy outcome. With mixture of a gentle, social life, there's nothing wrong in attending workshops together and learning and reading at this time, In fact, this is the best time to know what you prefer, and do it.

Source: Some words taken from the list, "From archangel Rapheal oracle deck book" by Doreen virtue. After all, she is carrying your baby, who is also hers, but is yours equally. Lots of encouragement. Gentle writer.

Activity for you: To go through it gracefully.

Its natural to care for each others
Harmony and health
Understanding
Sirname surrender and sleep
Becoming and blessings
Offspring and office
Nature and nurture
Dreams and depth and dance

Engagement and energy
Daily shares and structure
Security to surrender

Memories matter and money
Enthusiasm and embrace

A new beginning
Gifts and giving
Allowing love and aligning
Intrests and intuition

Relationships are also relation-shares,
relation care,(scare) relation love,
relation peace.
This is one area of life where we should not be
scared but imbibe the rest!

I am being contained in this baby's gentle love.
I am a container of our unique love.
I am being contained in my family's love,
I am being contained in God's love.

Be a container of your own love.

He won't let anything peel your integrity
He will truly fold it with care.
Where are such connections these days?
Don't say anything...
believe
because only you two breathe together
and give O2 to the relationship
than expecting others to save it for you.
Little by Little we let go of 'loss' but
never of 'love'

Changes

Creative, celebrative, caring, honest, humble, human, alive, assertive, alert, natural, newness now, guided gifts and great fullness, encouragement, support during changes bring in these qualities, or the opposite.

Gentle writer in me thinks...

Changes can bring up both qualities but when we gently realise we can face the upcoming changes with the power of togetherness, understanding, love, gentleness and listening. standing by with and for each other. The performance of the pregnancy test. The health provider visits. Any and all ultrasound sounds. Birth education classes. Any test procedures. The birth. The best is to be in tune with her through the process. Identify the support system that you can depend on when you feel depleted or any negative emotions. The gift of a pure hug.

A true hug feels like you've come home and it is heart: full, understanding and greatfullness the best hug is your presence during pregnancy, uncondtionally towards self and the inborn baby, and those who caretake for you!

'It's safe to be loved just as I am' family Culture and tradition and religion Our cultures and traditions take us back to remembering how to be and what to do than to always try to seek new solutions sometimes its wiser to go back to the old, the already tried and tested, the old rich roots of our culture they're there to guide, and we will always find a way.

I respect my culture and tradition and find ways to play the role in it the best respectful way I can. because its an honor to belong and be a beautiful part of a tradition and a privilidge.

Write down 10 things you appreciate about the culture you belong to

1)

2)

3)

4)

5)

6)

7)

8)

9)

10)

Relationship with money matters

We have to remove 'guilt' and fear' from earning Money or Wealth instead of worrying about this, we remember money is Lakshmi, but it is also Saraswati and Vishnu and Shiva which means it is important yet meant to be valued and enjoyed.

Beliefs like black money has all come out of spending it recklessly, and possessing and fearing. It is painful sometimes how we treat money.

But when we learn to trust... the day I realised my value for money, I had a realisation which I remember dawned on me, I started saving more stopped spending recklessly, started valuing exchanges, stopped demanding, instead learnt to work towards my talent and learnt to value my time and others. I had to remove the enemy of guilt and embrace the lightness of grace and enrichment with my relationship with money. I am sure everyone has had their breakthroughs in money. Its so important to value yours.

As an individual it is so important to improve your relationship with money, infact this is what will bring us back to honor and humility.

Read about the journeys of people who are earning and happy and content and full of love and light. Acknowledge the power of money, don't treat it too lightly, But also notice, When you don't allow good to flow to you beautifully because you are stuck in corruptness of money! Instead look at the +ives, it gives you shelter property you can own tools which matter to you.

You can make a career and enrich your world. You can invest in a talent and share with the world. You can do something you love without fear of security and you can feel freedom and joy in negative sides. You spend it just on pleasure.

To help your child better with money. Let them learn how to save money from the beginning make them aware of the value of their own time and energy, and others.

When people buy something from you, they buy from the 'hours of your life'

And then let go and see how they shape up. Only we are essentially responsible for our own wellbeing and exchanges.

Have gentle and Realistic expectations from children, unreal expectations attract Sucide rates, competition and so exchange carefully, with love and understanding'.

Best parent is the one who demonstrates this, and as we move about we try our best. I renew my relationship with money, and life.

Money

Mine ours never ending exchange yours. The importance of the above acronym means, that money is not just mine, it becomes ours, and yours is when we exchange it in dignity care, and remembering that it has value with the way we will choose to treat and exchange it with understanding and compassion.

Support and sharing

What I meant here by support is that everyones lifetime and experiences are different and unique, some go according to plan fortunately and some Don't, but what matters is having that shoulder strength and a caring connection/foundation to depend on in ones lifetime and experiences. We all have had our unique experiences that have made us either richer, or more poorer hungrier or content, stable or unstable,we all dance between these in our lives, what matters is we don't forget the who, how where and what we do our time energy and capacity.

That is why support and strength are sacred qualities of Divine just like when I think of Hanuman jee carrying a mountain on his palm, I think of loving parenting as trying to uplift their child, and that upliftment is sacred how we embrace that upliftment is up to us whether with an open heart and humbleness or a closed heart and Mind.

If I could see Lakshman's effort, I would see brotherhood and offering gentle companianship in my process

If I could see rams effort in every time someone would try to bring more peace harmony and joy and heroism in my life I would see ram in them.

If I could see shivas effort, upliftment is a quality we do everyday lets think of what all we uplift everyday.

When someone helps improve our mood. When someone compliments and means it truly. when someone blesses us and means it truly. When someone saves us from a negative association. When someone brings us good news.

- How can we give to each other?
- What is my unique quality?
- What do we learn from each other?
- What can we do to make it a better and more enriching experience for each other?
- What is the quality of our spending time together?
- Where do we want to go?
- And do we want to achieve?
- What is my role in this?

- Is the giving and receiving quality of all participants equal and happy?
- So, ask yourself these questions, are our roots going to be connected for a long time?
- Is there a long term with this group?
- What are we learning from each other?
- And don't see anyone as an enemy. Who triggers you, see their good side, in turn they will see yours.

Support

Support, understanding, patience, persistence, of real, rooted truth. Be real with each other, that is the point of having a support group.

Before the baby was born, the energy exchange was between the couple, now it's between the mom and baby. Then, it is between the baby and the world, and the immediate support system.

Having a support system is nourishing because, support means we know whom to trust and rely on, everyone cannot be our support, but a few can be, and at birth the support system is the following.

Identifying local options

Hospitals that are baby friendly
Labor doulas
Postpartum doulas
Chiropractors.
Mothers support groups.

Midwives Birth centers
Baby wearing resource
Car seat safety.

Spouse partner: They may have little or no knowledge of birth, but their being there is healthy, essential, and supportive for the pregnant wife/mother.

Family support: Family is often there as a part of their own life experience. They play a role in caring and giving intimate space, with family we share our intimate space and feelings, and often need their help to pass through the process.

Doctor: The doctor is typically not present throughout a woman's labor, and not able to coach her through labor. Doctors have office hours to keep, other woman in labor, and other issues that may keep them away from the woman. The doctor's essential role is to keep the integrity of the health checks for the mother, and inform the mother about her process, so it becomes successful.

Doula: A doula is someone who give objective and informational support to women giving birth, and immediate postpartum. They are trained in birth and remain objective, with a wealth of knowledge about the processes that occur in the body. They suggest relaxation techniques, support measures, labor positions and added support of birth.

Message to the reader

I am greatfull to my school Mgd for teaching me this prayer Humko mann ki shakti dena and it is also a song which is the beginning prayer of this chapter I used to sing it in school and I recalled it and added immediately in the book what bloomed into something beautiful was the poem Circle of love and belonging. It is about making everyday meaningful in ones own way and happy and I believe knowing whom we can turn our back to at the end of the day is Our circle of love and much more. This chapter would really gently open my heart gently whenever I would read it as a writer this chapter took a lot less time to structurize, because it was more poetic as relations are actually poetic and poetry is from the heart opposite of calculative ,This chapter is less factual so I had no idea how to put the information but as an author I knew ill come up with something right for my readers to enjoy and get enriched by. Whatever you turn your back on you will eventually have to face for the plain simple reason the world is round made me aware of something very important we cant ignore this area of life as it sets our foundation but also gives us an opportunity to bloom and make choices based on our heart I was also inspired by the eternity symbol. This chapter also talked about our support system and our closest ones we choose to grow with.

Quote to ponder: *"A family doesn't have to be perfect, it just needs to be united"*

- Whose goals matter the most in the home? Is everyone given equal opportunity to speak what matters to them?

- Who is in your circle of love and belonging? Can you open your home or heart for more? Or you are stamped and limited to only this?

- Whom out of your family members do you really enjoy growing with everyday in some way? Do you know how difficult it can be for someone to do a task that you can do so effortlessly?

Family affirmation: We are joy to depend on and with just like a bark of a tree my family and loved ones are a dependable support Life is ease on me and I am easy on life, life supports me and I support it back!

Notes

1. What were some of the favourite lines from this chapter. How did it make you Feel?

_____

_____

_____

_____

_____

_____

_____

_____

_____

2. What insights did you receive to make your experience more enriching and meaningful?

_____

_____

_____

_____

_____

_____

_____

_____

_____

Nurturing Chapter 4

Bringing up a Wise & Happy Child
The Lap of Love and Care

Throughout this chapter you will read practical tips on how to nourish your baby when he or she is born, if one already has a baby this chapter will help you improve the quality of care you will give your baby and if you are waiting for the baby this chapter will mentally and emotionally prepare you on how you could comfort and nourish and prepare for your baby's birth.

This chapter also talks about psychological aspects of the baby and us when they are born it is so important to prepare one self mentally and sensibly because logically the baby is going to try and be like you and initially and follow you and your lifestyle. we all hope to stay alive healthy and active, for long to be able to see our grandchildren and see their smiling happy faces, so hence it is so important to keep one self healthy happy, and active to live long, and attract strength to live a greatful life for the baby and your self and family.

The best words you'd want to hear from your childs mouth are' ***mom dad I had an amazing childhood***!

First words and first walk

The first time your child will talk or walk
The first time you spoke,
Notice the way you talk and walk now
And refresh it bring quality in it
Don't take your voice or communication or
granted either

The first time your child will talk or breathe,
will also, be the first time,
You remember the value of living.
Through his or her speech,
Don't take your breath for granted,
And others time,
Friendship efforts
Or even your time
Every second is like a heartbeat,
Every heartbeat is like life.

*Every new born that is born, teaches us that
life gives us beautiful precious chances. To
evolve, grow, relean and Be.*

Lesson

Focus on where you are making more than extra efforts
where you can relax you walk the extra mile looking
through their flaws and imperfections, and even your
own and offering your true care and friendship, notice
how much effort it takes to reach out to someone,
notice the little efforts your child is doing to reach out
to you when he or she is growing up and learning and
developing, also remember all the steps you have taken
so far and remember to remind yourself your every little
walk, when it is more conscious becomes beautiful than
unconscious.

I respect and cherish my unique able inner child.
Notice if you are aware of how you walk whether you have
any life or beauty in where you are going or you are just
dragged into it,

All this will affect how your child will learn to walk
talk and be we all have not always walked our talk or
talked our walk and its fine god has not sent me to earth
to make it perfect! I am here so I can learn and walk
through perfections and notice how where my joy lives
and breathes naturally.

Also notice how you ignore your time to relax and
bombard it with activities that aren't really nourishing
or helpful.

Common fears of toddlers- Loud noises, Strangers and separation. Obviously the period from infancy to toddlerhood they will face loud noises of the world, and will see strangers and experience separation but it is so essential for the parent not to become a child and fearful, an adult needs to help the child walk and enjoy the world eventually.

Stranger anxiety can be cured, with looking at it logically and rationally, the child who learns to see logically and rationally wont let this fear burden or grow in him/her.

Don't we remember the days we could not walk?

Help them deal with their fears ' gently' and gradually by, showing them that the world is a gentle and loving place, and help them experience it for themselves, their curiosity is what will make them grow if they are curious, invite them to gently learn add fullstop after them.

Isn't it fun to see the world from a Childs perspective?

Fresh, full of joy, possibility and goodness. You want to hear them say one day,

Mom dad I had a wonderful childhood!
And you tell the child,
Well you created all of it!

A friendly infant or toddler learns to understand emotions and bonds with them accordingly, with reverence and empathy the gift of Care.

Gratitude for care

Are you smiling?

When you give birth,
You are gifting yourself
with your soul's truest care and creativity,
Care is so sacred,
embrace it and nurture and recognize and
realize the gift of it,
and allow it to grow
give it a foundation of your inner strength.

When your love and care are running dry
either they aren't nourished,

or have been drained.
True care gives you strength, and
courage to face
the realisation of what
living without it would feel.
Even scared has
'care' in it
and sacred
has acre, which if you twist around
You'll make 'care'
Care is
Watch your acre of care we try
To extend our care everywhere
It first begins by tending to our own
garden of our heart,
Before spreading it too thin around,
It's natural to reach out
Are we reaching out properly?
Are we reaching in gently too?
Or just reaching out all the time?
Care, aligned, recreating, embrace.
If your child has learnt to 'care'
in their heart for somebody or something,
a vision, a person, a project, a passion, a cause.
You will have succeeded.

Written on 2018 April

Smile
Surrender my intuition loving embrace/e
nrichment

Surrender my intentions lovingly embrace.

Care brings us in touch with our smile love and
intuition.

The smile

During your pregnancy make it a habit to smile
with your whole body mind and heart.
Its called the ''Heart smile'

Playing with your baby

Playing with the baby is meant to be fun light and is often
interactive so its so important for the parent to be aware
on how to play safely and consiously.

Play can be progressive playful loving light make sure
your baby has enough space to crawl give your baby a
few toys and opportunity to learn that her and his actions

have effects for example when she drops a toy and it falls to the ground.

Use a mirror to show your baby different facial expressions. Walking, jumping usually starts from 1 to 3 years. Limit screen time, your own or your child's, as they grow older real time social interactions are much better than screen all time screen playing and it keeps their senses Fit.

Take care of yourself, playing with your toddler takes in energy, however it gives you an opportunity to stay youthful. Other toys that toddlers enjoy include:

- brightly colored balls
- blocks, stacking and nesting toys
- fat crayons or markers
- age-appropriate animal or people figures and dolls

- toy cars and trains
- shape sorters, peg boards
- simple puzzles
- push, pull, and riding toys

Some nonverbal signs children share

When they are happy with a certain activity or play or focus involvement or interaction.

- They show signs of wanting to do it often
- They will be happy with exploring it more,
- but you have to teach the child,
- They literally share joy on the plate,

- and laughter when in front of the activity.
- These are aspects of development which develop in them.

Physical (doing) When a child enjoys an activity socially, he will want to become even better at it, best is to him find his motive or intention, than just pleasing others' mostly kids learn with experimenting here, some kids are more determined.

When a toddler or a child find themselves in activities which are not for them they can cry or show signs of uneasiness, in these situations help them by lifting them and placing them in activities which they enjoy and even in school they will have to choose subjects which they don't enjoy because it is compulsory, so they have to be a little adapting to the systems of the world, hence help them develop a talent as they grow up instead of letting them get inside the blame game ' I don't like school' situations.

By doing normal daily activities instead of just mental, or just superficial, they need balance of all. in their developing process.

- They need these three aspects in their learning process

- To grow and move through life, social, emotional and mental,

- They learn by doing, some learn by interacting some learn superficially and some are deeper learners whatever style they develop they are choosing but you have to help them with a holistic question, are you enjoying what you are involved, doing learning and interacting with?

- Can you relate with it?

Developing coordinating skills

When they play games, or will take part in sports or do schoolwork coordination Excercises are important for your child. Coordination usually means whether the the child can do various coordination movements effectively. In a effective way.

Developing visual motor integration: Known as VMI. Is an effective, efficient communication between the visual system and the motor systems. Good VMI skills can help your child correctly copy to draw the shapes, numbers and letters that he / she sees, which is helpful in developing their handwriting skill.

Visual perception: Visual perception activities helps children to make sense of the information that the eyes are sending to the brain. Having good visual perception skills can therefore help prepare your child for the future in visual activites.

Visual discrimination: good visual discrimination can help a child perceive letters and numbers where there is a small difference between them (Egg 5 and 5)

Hand dominanace: Hand dominance is a hand preference that refer to a persons, consistent use of one hand rather than the other hand for skilled task. The more a child uses a specific hand for a task, the more stronger that hands dominance becomes.

More ON child development

Child development is a process every child goes through, there are five types of development they experience quite naturally.

Cognitive: Childs ability to solve problems. Including helping themselves and self control.

Social and emotional development: this is the Childs ability to interact with others, including helping themselves and self control.

Speech and language development: this is Childs ability to understand and use language.

Fine motor skill development: this is the Childs ability to use small muscles pick up objects hold a spoon..

Gross motor skill development: this is the Childs ability to use muscles.

What is a developmental milestone?

A developmental milestone is a skill that a child acquires within a specific time frame. One developmental milestone is learning to walk most children learn this skill at the age of 9 to 15 months.

Milestones for three months

Raises head and chest when lying on stomach. Supports upper body with arms and lying on stomach. Opens and shuts hands. Pushes down on legs when feet are placed on a firm surface brings hand to mouth.

Visual milestones

Watches face intently follows moving objects. Recognizes familiar objects and people at a distance smiles at the sound of a voice begins to imitate some sounds.

Social and emotional milestones

Begins to develop a social smile. Becomes more communicative and expressive with face and body imitates facial movements

Milestones

I respect life and I respect my baby's to be lifetime, this makes me have patience love and care for myself and them.

"Fun is meant to be fresh, fullfilling, understanding and new and nurturing, and filled with loving focus never ferocious and naive. Or foolish intrusive or insensitive."

"In a world of insensitive intrusions,the best gift we give to children is to help them build their joy day by day, to make it a foundation for all opposites they will see in the world, and turn back to the joy."

The world is how we are

Infants hardly feel any unease in their little bodies, well because their tiny stomach's are relaxed and in flow of wellbeing naturally but as infants become toddlers and start growing up that is when they need most interaction, play and even guidance about what is good and not good play, and this way they wont make the same mistakes twice and wont get into experiences for the play or temporary pleasure of it but they will regain their little strength and discipline and learn to gather themselves than lose or forget their own center or emotions.

Its natural to move into a world of so much entertainment and get lose or lose yourself, but to do anything with lack of enjoyment is boring, Learning is also meant to be enjoyable, and it is the way it is, one has to adjust in all types of environment to thrive and survive happily. Some children imbibe quickly some take time but they all want to thrive. Some children are ok to play as long as they can interact with the material and quality does not matter. Some children like to know what they are playing with.

How we introduce playing for children, helps them form images about what they can play with, and what they cant as they grow up.

As they will learn rules in school, to help them with the world, a parent one can need to build a healthy foundation of balanced indoor and outdoor play for the child, This will help the child, gain the best from both types of playing. And will have a balanced mindset.

Clingy offers a gift

The hidden gift is a conscious contact / caring / connected / loving interested nurturing Gifted / guided you And baby. Let it teach you compassion and help the baby adapt more properly by you being an example.

Don't reject a clingy baby but see it as a loving partnership and give this relationship priority and affection and respect.

How?

Remind the child that they can learn these qualities from you, and learn to cultivate in them as they are growing up. Then we have a mature relationship with attachment and warmth in our future relationships.

The first time an infant is born they need skin contact of a mother, and thereafter they will learn to connect/ contact/ communicate with the world, and surrounding and find their space and role in it.

Let them enjoy social functions without your constant narration or need to be clinged on to you. Treat them as normal children don't label or judge them see something positive socially in them or make them aware of a good habit they do.

To help bring up a caring autonomic individual a child learns these qualities of care love interest nurturing, from you the most and what is around them Babies reveal their feelings, the way you reveal them. So be conscious and caring about how you reveal your feelings and emotions. Clingy babies are not going to be clingy forever, but its important to notice that they know and feel that their feelings are respected and so are their needs. When they receive your attention and contact with out distraction They will value being with you.And develop into healthy autonomic individuals Who are capable of giving receiving love in a healthy way and not a clingy manner. Most babies take their first steps sometime between **9** and **12**months and are walking well by the time they're **14** or **15 months** old. Don't worry if your child takes a little longer, though. Some perfectly normal children don't walk until they're **16** or **17** months old. Don't force the child into any behavior, keep it gradual notice their routine and help accordingly.Children learn to adapt naturally and instinctually.

Healthy ways to cope with grief or depression

Talk to a therapist. Listen intently have patience with your healing process. Never isolate yourself because of shame. Bounce back with exercise activity and self care. Detox when you can and build strength in your close friendships and circle.

Its safe to rely on each other for strength. Its safe to recognize to never make anyone my pillar of hope and depend totally on them. Its safe to recognize and remember I am part of this beautiful world and there is enough to heal with and from.

When anyone you know is experiencing these attributes, remember to teach them to forgive themselves and say the hopononopo prayer

- *I love you*
- *I forgive you*
- *Thank you*
- *Im sorry.*

This will immediately remind them to focus

Its safe to be seen

Its safe to be loved and to be interested.
Its safe to be interesting in my own way.
Its safe to nurture and be nurtured
Its safe to see the day as new.

Listening takes skill if we can listen with love interest and see the person in the moment engage, get enriched and enthuse with the listening, Learn something new, be in the now and learn a nurturing perspective, we are listening well.

Also it is so important to avoid distractions as much as you can; empathizing and listening to the whole sentence before interupting.'

Good gentle listening and bonding flourish in environment where togetherness, bonding and expression are possible where like minded people are present, and there are no intruders or distractions. Or too much information. Where hearts can bond, there is realistic sharing and honesty policy always. honest communication and interpersonal skills, never makes you lose focus on the bigger picture and get clouded with other peoples details of the present.

You can only truly listen to someone you can see be in the now with, be truthful with, and can be affected by their enthusiasm and enrichment.

Everything else is just information, flattery and praise. Importance of the way we use 'words is so essential because the way we use words towards ourselves and our toddlers shows what we believe about our world view, and life in general. We can take it as a growing relationship, where we learn to grow and enrich ourselves about the world, improve our world view than give in to criticism. **'Children are not things to be folded but people to be unfolded.'**

Why do children start lying?

Children start lying when they hold in secretive desires but feel shy to pursue them, they are too bind by 'I cant do it' to move into 'I can' and they need help to find their truth, in this case its important to understand how they are perceiving life, what they are liking and really getting close to the child and his likes dislikes and interests, helping them to improve on their strengths makes them wiser to not shy or hide or suppress heir weaknesses. They stop lying when they are heard, when someone believes in them, when they have a positive role model, and their actions are filled with grace and freshness.

Below you will see certain dialogues parents have with their children, sometimes the children catch up to words, but if you develop your empathy, you will notice that the parent is speaking from care or either they really want to say something to you, that the wise parent is speaking from loving concern and their true feelings.' A teenager will listen differently, a toddler will listen differently, depending on each persons temperment, I remember as a teenager, I found sitting and listening to be the tuffest, but having a desire to lend a respectful and a nonjudgemental ear is a blessing on each, and visa versa the parent can bring a child into a good communication space and likewise.

Be quiet	Can you use a kinder/ softer voice ?	Be quiet is more in-structional, and we were used to hearing in schools, but when we talk to our babies often we should be softer.

What a mess!	Its time to clean up	This tells a baby that they are the ones who are wrong to make a mess, its only natural not to know how to clean up, lets clean or time to clean up is better to use.!
I explained how to do it yesterday	Maybe i can show you another way. Or you show me your way?	You can always show again.
Stop crying	Its ok to Cry sometimes.	Same as be quiet
Its not that hard.	you can always try if really want to.	You can always try sounds more inspiring and motivating, than saying its not that hard.

It really matters how they say , what they say, where they say,because a child is also a conscious being'

Relaxed empathy

Health care professionals have to practice empathy a lot, they can have a compassion fatigue which means they need to recharge their own selves more often than normal professionals. Imagine, listening to patients stories, of pain, tremor, and many others unless a person is not strong the person can have fatigue resulting disorders.

'This goes for both the parents and chidlren, we all need a gentle break to unwind and connect beautifully again'

Hence go on a Empathy fast for a week, why are holidays there? Because we need a break but instead of holiday you can respect your sensitivity and receptivity and remember it is there for a purpose that you will understand. Your sensitivity and receptivity is a beautiful gift that should be respected, and channeled correctly. Otherwise you can absorb everything and emphathize unconsiously which is draining and not good for your health as well empathetic sensitive and caring parents usually have empathetic sensitive and caring children.

I am empathetic in a balanced manner. I respect my ability to understand I remember not to over empathize. I can learn to relax and remember I am doing the best I am doing with what I have right now.

Memory and you

Some amazing facts about the brain.

Did you know?

The brain has powers to mend damage after stroke. Cuddling a baby encourages it to grow. Physical affection causes the brain to secrete a chemical called dopamine which in turn triggers the release of growth hormones, babies deprived of close physical contact or affection develop less happily.

The brain is the fastest growing organ in the body. So you only have to remain healthy, in diet exercise and routine to give birth to a baby with a healthy brain. And be aware of stimulants.

The brain is able to alter any physical function. – heart rate can be slowed, bowed relaxed and blood vessel opened or closed. Just through thought. imagining being warm, for example can increase temperature in a persons fingers more than 1 degree Celcius.

No two brains are identical. So when you tell someone use your brain or think like me, you are not giving good advice. We already use our brain, but yes we learn from each other, but our brain does not change its basic structure. Each fetus experiences different stimuli and nutrients.

A happy brain can help fight gut infections.. The body's immune system responds directly to changes in the brain also a sad event, such as losing a loved ones, can produce depletion in the number of infection fighting cells within days.

During childbirth the mothers brain is flooded with hormone that helps the mother child bond and dull the memory of the pain as giving birth can be painful, one reason is that the memory of pain is wiped out by the hormone oxytocin whch rebuilds more cells after birth. Depression is caused when the mother is stuck in the after memory of the pain, than moved on from it she didn't give her self time to process the grief is she lost a child as well.

Storage overload When we learn information but don't put in practical use.

Storage failure When our brain does not want to store more information

Here the brain can feel overwhelmed

Stop. So in pregnancy avoid the above, storage failure or overload. Because that means you aren't emotionally present with what is happening to and around you, don't let pregnancy weaken your memory, but actually make it stronger and that is possible.

Did you know?

Dental hygiene naturally boosts your memory when bacteria collects in the mouth it sends inflammation through out the body and even the brain.

Have this memory smoothie

- Carrot
- Blueberry
- Almonds
- Fresh ginger
- Avocado.
- Beetroot.

Mix them together and enjoy the delicious memory enhancing smoothie its natural to have litle memory lapses when you are pregnant, its because of the little life forming inside you, and the energy it requires, however, being gentle and relaxing is the key.

Pay attention to little things of your life that are only your Business and not everyone else's business its natural to want to forget the pain of your pregnancy and start feeling the joy of giving birth and that shows that the woman had less depression and was more active.

How good is your episodic memory?

Episodic memory is highly subjective and may depict or predict your future behavior it goes in a sequence and it is impactful and present in mostly all our relationships, so we should take care of this as this creates our daily experience of life.

Visual memory is depicted by smells and sounds and visuals of what happened in the memory. Usually we tend to remember according to the quality of our attention.

This can help you to understand yourself better and bring more awareness to your present moments. And more quality

- What did you have for breakfast this morning?
- What did you have for breakfast yesterday?
- What did you have for lunch day before yesterday?

- What did you have for breakfast this day two years ago?
- How did you celebrate your last birthday?
- When was the last time you ate chocolate?
- Why when was the last time you cried?
- When and where was the last time you drank a cup of coffee?
- Can you remember an occasion of a child you felt really proud?
- When you make a gentle effort to remember this your brain will function sharp and good enough for you to enjoy your present moments even more to the fullest.

Care for your senses

Care for your eyes

Put rose water with cotton bud on your eyes often use eye drops while travelling or when in a environment with toxicity. Use protection glasses be aware of UV radiation from technology the Aritificial light is harmful for the eyes. Look at natural light.

Care for your nose

Remember the good smells that you truly enoyed smelling and gave you good energy. Clean your nose. Put cotton bud in your nose before sleeping if you catch lots of cold and cough. Use clove oil whenever the nose is distressed.

Care for your ears

Use acupressure buttons for your ears. Use ear buds. Clean your ears give your listening a break respect your listening listen to calming sounds of nature. Respect your attention span.

Your favorite smells	Your favorite tastes	Your favorite sight	You favorite sounds

Lets talk a little about their little gentle developing mind and body. Girls bodies develop their muscles more slowly than boys.

What it means to be a girl?

Nurturing abilities are developing, is also a desire to nurture and identify with what is mine. This develops in both the sex, but girls more quickly.

Listening abilities are developing, being a great listener is a desire to listen in a heart smart way. Every person carries these desires which form their attitudes towards life from early on.

For both the sexes body image is developing to help them with this, smile at them when you see them and touch them lovingly, and always with dignity.

Self image is developing : always say well done when they do something which they truly like.

Some basic biological differences in men/women	girls voices are thinner
Boys voices are heavier	Women don't grow sharp hair on their faces called beard, except they grow normal facial hair but not as heavy as beard.
Boys grow hair on their faces	
Boys naturally have different structure of bones.	Girls naturally have a different structure of bones.
Boys have little difference in skin texture.	Girls have softer skin.

They want to understand the world around them and what feels good, guide them healthfully towards healthier options. They want to understand their developing selves, so getting them involved with them in different types of activities, and also find out what they 'enjoy' and value slowly.

They want to bond with others, help them with social building activities so they learn to respect, and learn interpersonal or intrapersonal skills.

Nature tends to move towards loving caring balance. Don't force them into any attitude or activity that they don't feel good in, You can find this with the way they react or respond."

Affirmations for the growing up toddler

I let go of stress regarding my child interaction socially with the world now. I trust my child will be wise socially. I believe I can bring up healthy adults. I trust my child will develop their abilities with their own interests.

I believe they will choose the right interests for them, and if not their sadness will take them to joy in their days I am sure these above advises on being interested in their interests noting their strengths, and teaching them to be socially wise, will teach your toddlers to be smart individuals in the world, and feel good enough to pursue and not be shy about their gentle developing selves.

Obviously till the time they are developing they are dependent but you can show them glimpses of what it means to be an adult as they move through their teens, this will build them up for life.

However right now we are just talking about infancy and toddlerhood and stranger anxiety but if the stranger anxiety does not pass on to adult hood, make sure it is well taken care of since toddlerhood itself.

Babies teach us that a new world is possible with their freshness and the beauty of the divine they bring to the planet, they bring in a gift, which must be nurtured, protected, cherished and shaped in the right way as much as possible.

Different type of dominant learning styles

Verbal: Linguistic Sensitive to the meaning and order of words.

Musical: Sensitive to pitch melody rhythm and tone.

Logical: Mathamatical able to handle chains of reasoning and recognise patterns and order.

Spatial: Is the capacity to understand, reason and remember the spatial relations between objects or space., Visual spatial abiltites are used everyday, from understanding or fixing equipment.

Body Kinesthetic: Able to use the body skill fully and handle objects.

Interpersonal: Understand people or relationships.

And intrapersonal: Possess access to ones emotional life as a means to understand oneself and others.

affirmation for growing up toddler: we let of stress regarding our child growing up in the world, wisely, I beelive they will be healthy, and will develop interests and abilities at their own pace"

Find out which one of these is your toddler being drawn towards. Some children may demonstrate qualities of all these in little forms, and some may display just one or two, whatever is right for the child he will have more **'interest'**.

Remember interest is Investing intuition now time engaged remember enrich see trust/ try again and will want to do often.

Whatever they will have an interest in is what they will invest, be joyfully engaged with will also care to remember will be enriched and will enrich, they will see often and will trust and turn to.

I hope they learn to polish the gifts that truly matter and not run after flattery and fake praise.

I hope she learns quickly the difference between false and true.

And so, it is, and it is so. When worries turn into belief, and faith turns into friendship and passion turns into progress, and love turns more into loving and being loved, we are learning to live and learn more meaningfully. Slowly but surely or quickly and now. Time is now.

Also A tip,

Keep a toddler dairy: Note down their development progress and remember to make positive notes for them so they can learn to accept their strengths with pride and not hide their weaknesses but improvise on them.

Give them hugs often. Because too much criticism but gentle correction is needed always clouds their perception towards graceful development.

"Pure love and compassion is matchless in Majesty, it has no parellel power, and no darkness can match its loving purity."

Bonding and breastfeeding

Mantra for knowledge, divinity, wisdom, memory, and creativity. Aum saraswati vidmahe riye dhi mahi Tanno saraswati prachodayat.

What is colostrum?

Colostrum is the yellow milk, rich in protein, antibodies vitamins and minerals. Transitional milk is thin and white and contains high quantities of fat,calories protein and vitamins. Finally transitional milk is replaced by the production of mature milk, consists mainly of water and will appear blush in color when first expressed. This is called Foremilk. And then it transforms into hind milk, which is filled with nutrients. There is nothing called as weak or bad breast milk its just the diet and freshness and fluid intake which determines the quality of the breast milk of the mother. Milk is holy, it's the first contact with the mother.

Breastfeeding fears

Engorgement presents itself as a very real possibility for every lactating woman, this painful condition occur when a woman's breasts become overfull with milk. The breast and Areola may feel hard swollen and warm and the skin may stretch and appear shiny.

You may experience tenderness in the breasts, and Under arm area or run a low grade fever. This condition can occur in the areola and body of either one or both breasts. Build to a peak before decreasing, remain at the same level for an extended period of time or even peak several times!

Solution massage the breasts

You can even use a cool compress on the breast to relive the tension. Avoid excess stimulation of the affected breast for breast avoid extended heat and pumping sensation, and do not restrict your fluid intake. Stay well hydrated as limiting fluids will not aid in eliminating engorgement breast milk changes, so If you see a change in it don't worry it is part of lactating!

How long to breastfeed?

Some mother feed for 1 year and 8 months, some for 2 and some for 3 years.

Plugged milk duct

A plugged milk duct is blocked milk duct is an area of the breast, where milk flow is obstructed. This is caused by when a milk duct is blocked you may notice, a decrease in your milk secretion. But with frequent nursing and pumping sessions and massage sessions this problem will normally relax as your condition improves. It is important that one does not stop nursing.

Supportive measures for healthy breast feeding

Get plenty of rest. Drink fluids Eat nutritious foods to aid your immune system. Nursing management. Before nursing apply a warm compress and gently massage the breast. Loosen your bra and wear non restrictive clothing to aid in milk flow. Apply gentle breast massage or compressions while nursing. Massage breasts with coconut oil, and vinegar to cure itchy nipples.

Breastfeeding and bonding

The caring drops of love Imagine your babe is latching on to your breasts holistically and lovingly, and when he or she does your heart sings as every drop of milk touches their lips the pleasure-able sensations that run through your body are of joy gladness and sense of loving accomplishment.

Some women cannot breast feed their baby, they have to take help of other mothers or feed them bottle milk, but if one has to choose those options or You can feel your baby, its a gift and a moment of love between you too, so enjoy it now. You are less exhausted, you are free of fatigue now, You are enjoying the sacred skin to skin contact with your baby Her or his skin feels like the kindest velvet to your skin,And as this contact is made, You feel a sense of 'bond; developing between you and your baby. You are supporting the baby's body at the moment, His or her wellbeing is the moments wish, Enjoy the flow of wellbeing through your milk Feeding the baby, Feel like you are the container of loving manna of flow for your baby, See your smile of the day becoming even bigger and warmer As you are doing the act.

In fact this is the moment when lots of mothers, acclaim falling in love, with their baby.

Isnt that precious?

Feed your own skin in a precious way Feed your skin fabrics of comfort and kindness, Gentle and cheerful Affirmation for breastfeeding. Feeding my child is a holy activity. My feeding environment is nurturing, smoke free, stress free, infection free intruder free.

Confidently breastfeeding

My gentle mind thinks.. breastfeeding come from your wings, and nourishment comes from your roots, and how you allow yourself to be treated. So, make sure to let yourself receive love and affection. Keep your phones and laptops far away. Have music playing in the background. Have gentle images around you.

Fact: Breastfeeding is not supposed to hurt. If it hurts, please consult a doctor. Meanwhile enjoy these extra recipes for breastfeeding. Every one wants a attractive baby you just want a happy loving and divine baby. Happiness is naturally attractive and Divine.

What makes you truly happy?

In Indian history Yashodha ma and Krishna has been shown in history as a perfect and divine combination, is Krishna happy? Is Yashodha happy? Is all we have to ask.

The beautiful formed lips to the perfect eye sight, all is a result of good actions and thoughts today, now not in some future. For happiness now we need to think and be happy now. And then it shows.

Baby's skin and senses

The earliest sense to form in babies is the sense of touch Embreyo's about 1 month can sense touch to their noses and lips, the ability spreads quickly and nearly the entire surface of the skin is sensitive to touch by 12 Weeks of age.

Sense of touch

This can actually regulate the body temperature. *Wearing your baby in a soft carrier,* where she is in an upright position, it's a sure way to keep her close all day. Did you know? When your baby is about 8 months, they can actually differentiate between a familiar object and an unfamiliar object. They explore with their hands and create a mental image of the object. But, their first contact is always through, their flesh, and first sense that is activated is **'touch'**

An infants ability to process visual information is not complete until several months after birth

Sight: Can babies see in the womb? Thats tough question to answer mostly because vision is our most complex sense, vision starts developing about four weeks after conception. The fetus forms little eye dots on either side of her tiny head. When the retina is being formed the brain is forming about 10 billion new synapses everyday. You would think the baby would get a migraine. One result of all this activity is that the neural circuitry necessary to control blinking, dilation of pupils, or tracking moving objects is present even before birth.

Do you know this song was originally created in 1818, By Franz Xaver Gruber' in a small town, called Salzburg Austria.

Hearing: in a study conducted in the book, brain rules for the baby the babies heard tapes of their mothers reading the cat in the hat while in the womb on a different story. Sucking rates and patterns were measured at all points.

The cellular function of smelling, appears as early, as the fourth week of fetal life

Smell: Just five weeks after fertilization you can see the brains complex wiring for smell. At first babies suffer from an acutely sensitive nose.

Taste: The tissues that mediate 'don't emerge from your embreyos tiny tounge Until about 8 weeks after conception. This does not mean the baby acquires the ability to taste something. That doesn't happen until third trimester. What you eat during the last trimesters can affect, the food preferences of your baby mildly.

How to prevent infant death syndrome in infants

Sudden infant death also called as cot death or crib death, is defined as sudden death of an infant that is unexpected.

It is more common in male babies, babies of teenage mothers babies born to mothers with lower rates in education or too instable situations to have a baby. It is common in premature babies, and formula fed babies than in breastfed babies. Vaccination is the most preventable and healthy breastfeeding but newborn care can prevent this infant death syndrome.

Baby stuff

Having a baby means buying the equipment.

What all do we need?

This crib is sometimes placed right next to your bed Try purchasing an organic mattress crib.

Baby sling: These are great for carrying small babies and there are many designs available. Make sure that whatever you purchase has a good buckle, or clasp that Will not slip out.

Changing table: you will need a safe place to change baby. Many moms have successfully used in kitchen or bathroom covered with towel. But if you can afford a changing table, with a strap to hold baby in buy all means purchase one.

Infant seat: you will find an infant seat extremely value-able, piece of equipment for babies up to about 6 months old. They allow baby to observe Household activities from a sitting up position.

Baby toilet trainer: a baby toilet trainer is essential and helpful for toilet training.

Your child will signal with crying or unease in face expression when his or her diaper is wet and soiled. Your child seems interested in Potty chair or toilet. Your child says that he would like to go to potty. Your child pulls his pants down then up again.

Clothing

keeping it simple and pure, purchase clothing that is chemical free as possible, and wash with organic detergent.

Choose your baby's clothing carefully. Currently all sleep wear for babies sized twelve months, and up that is not snug fitting or cotton, or treated with flame retardants Choose fabric that is bamboo or organic cotton.

Sunlight

Babies love the sunlight, fresh air. As they are growing they will act funny even weird, they need stimulation, discovery, some babies need novelty and mystery. some babies are ok with a simple and fresh routine. But all babies love sunlight, well some might not love it that much, but exposure to sunlight is essential and gives babies skin nutrients and loving gentleness.

Comforting your baby

When should I hold or comfort my baby?

You will normally hold your baby in your arms for many hours each day, as you care for your baby, feed your baby, holding him comes naturally,flirt with the baby, rock him in your arms, parent sing songs, all parents have a desire to bond with the infant, but the best bonding the of infant is with his own quick developing body, hence, the baby can get comforted from? What type of comfort are you offering the baby? A diaper change will comfort a wet baby, a feeding will comfort a hungry baby, holding will comfort a startled baby and sleep will comfort a tired baby, right, a baby can receive comfort in so many other ways such as being rocked, sung to, or taken for a stroll and being near music. Let him get comforted with life itself.

As we cradle, you we discover what true closeness feels like, How it blooms every day and becomes from painful to joyful, difficult to happy days.

Sleeping with joy with your baby

Sleep strategies for your baby

Sleeping schedules

At 2 months babies average 15.5 hours of sleep over a 24 hour period. 9.5 during night and 5 during naps. At six months of age, babies sleep 14.5 hours with 11 at night 3.5 during nights. At one year, babies sleep 14 hours of sleep, 11.5 at night and 2.5 during night.

Sleep little baby, in sweet possibility
you are cradled into the arms of the mother
and father, earth
stay comforted little baby,
May your original innocence and love rest,
and not be troubled by the world's woes at
this time'

may you sleep deeply,
little baby.
Because the quality of your sleep
determines
the health and wealth of your life experience.
Sleep little baby.
Wake up gently!
oops! Sometimes cooing and crying!

Sleep states of the newborn

Quiet alert: During the first hour of life, the newborn experiences this state, the baby is awake, alert and noticing the enviroment. It is optimal for the baby to be with his or her mother during this time, and for breastfeeding to be initiated.

Light sleep: The baby is sleeping lightly, which means he can be roused out of sleep, and may show jerky movements, sucking motions or even facial expressions.

Deep sleep: The baby Is sleeping very deeply, but may have small movements. But is difficult to arouse. He or she is quiet and unresponsive.

Silent Night

Silent night, holy night!
All is calm, all is bright.
Holy infant so tender and mild,
Sleep in heavenly peace,
sleep in heavenly peace and grace

Song from
A popular Christmas Carol.

Ways to make sleep work for the baby

During the day allow plenty of sunlight into the house or take him outside Put your baby down for day time or naps in a dark room. Strategically: darkness triggers the brain to release melatonin, a key sleep hormone. Keep your baby's days bright and his nights dark and he will quickly figure out when it's time to sleep. It's fine to use a night light but choose a small dim one that stays cool to the touch. If your child wakes up during the night, To induce night-time, sleepiness, consider installing dimmers on the lights, in your baby's room. But also in other rooms where you both spend a lot of time. Lower the lights in the evening to set the mood. Also try playing soothing music, infants do respond to relaxing music till toddlerhood for sleep.The baby responds and loves the mother or fathers voice, so consider basking shh to them if they don't fall asleep, or waking them up with your gentle voice, they will respond well. Consider finding instrumental, harp or piano.If early morning sunlight prompts your child to wake up too early, or if he has trouble napping in the afternoon consider installing room darkening shades.

Tip: 'Melatonin vitamin supplments can help the mother to sleep better and richer'

Try not to look your baby in the eye., As Many babies are easily stimulated: just meeting your baby's gaze can engage her attention to signal it is playtime or day time. Parents who make contact with sleepy babies encourage them to snap out of their sleep zone. The more joyful and soothing the interaction that takes place between your baby and you during the night, the more motivation they have to get up.

Don't worry if the baby wants to feed before sleeping for some infants that's a way to be soothed.Give your baby a gentle massage on toes or ankles before sleeping, with ghee or olive or coconut oil is the best option.

Intention- To love and honor the service others provide for us.

The mama papa song

It's so true, isn't it?
Everything I do, I do it for you.
What I eat, I do it for you,
What I earn, I do for you.
Where I breathe, I do it for you,
What I create, I do it for you.
What I touch, I do it for you
Everything I do, I do it for you.

Intention- To honor the intimate giving and receiving I share with life and others.

Babies cry because they are learning to adjust to the new environment so the more 'sorted you are', in the sense you aren't distracted, or too scattered the more,happily your babies will adjust to the surrounding But yes, of course you are the one who controls the surrounding while your baby is learning developing and adjusting.

Try Playing it back: When babies cry as toddlers, record their video or on the phone, and make them listen to it. When they hear it, so they can learn to laugh more quickly than they cry.

Laugh a lot: Make sure the baby listens to playful laughs on YouTube, or laugh a lot with the baby, with your whole self, you can only laugh if you feel light and happy.

Sing it back: Sing a song with the baby, this can rest the baby.

Chant it back: Chant OM sounds, Make them hear bird sounds.

Play instrumental music: when the baby is asleep-relaxed harp or piano. Change the scenery, take the baby to another room, another scenery that can make the experience better for the baby. Even adults do it, we need holidays, we need different surroundings. Moreover, a new location does make the baby change its moods.

Did you know?

Facts

Welcoming traditions around the world.

Japan: It is good to make space for the baby in the most nourishing ways in the home. Well in Japan, they store the umbilical cord in a wooden box. It is said that preserving the umbilical cord helps establish a good relationship between the child and mother. Well, who knew the mysteries of this culture?

Sweden: Outdoor napping for babies (Denmark and Sweden). Would you put your baby in the freezing cold for their lunchtime nap? Most Nordic parents would not give it a second thought. For them it's part of their daily routine. This is due to the fact that cold air actually helps babies sleep and eat better. Well, who knows? Just don't let the baby freeze. Almost all daycare centers in Denmark and Sweden believe this.

Finland: Every new born gets a maternity package from the government.(Finland). This is nice. Every new born gets gifts from the government, how kind! And what a way to welcome a new baby. Well, let's see what is included in the package. Clothes, sheets, toys. Mothers have a choice between taking a box or cash grant, which is currently a set worth 140 euros. All babies in Finland get a fresh and equal share of life!

Egypt: Place the baby in a large sieve and shake it up to help the newborn get accustomed to the vagaries of life (Egypt).

Armenia: Place a baby on the floor surrounded by symbolic items in order to know their future.(Armenia). When a baby gets his first tooth, Armenian parents celebrate with a ceremony called 'agra hading'. They place the baby on the floor surrounded by symbolic items such as a tape measure, a stethoscope,a spatula, a book and other objects. Parents then encourage the baby to choose one of these articles.

China: The baby's parents give outeggs that are dyed red, symbolizing happiness and renewal of life.(China). In china, when the baby turns one month old, the full moon ceremony is conducted to commemorate the first full month of life. On this morning, the baby's 30th day,relatives and friends gather to give their blessings and gifts for the new baby. In Chinese culture, eggs are the symbol of the wholeness of life.

Jamaica: The after birth, and cord are buried in a special location, and a tree is planted on the spot (Jamaica). I found this very amazing and evolutionary. It is interesting that every man should plant a tree, have a child, and write a book. In Jamaica parents only need to write a book, since the rest is already done! Well, in Jamaica the mother gives birth, the afterbirth and the cord are buried in a special location, and a tree is planted on that spot. The tree is provided by parents, godparents, and relatives. The tree is a pedagogical tool which teaches the child to take responsibility in life, since it is used to show the child that this is the beginning of his life and he must take care of it.Well, talk about 'planting', planting should be a part of every family's life! It's so important and sacred! This tradition comes from the Jamaican expression, home is where your navel string is buried. I think it means having a connection with your roots is essential.

Bali: Babies feet cannot touch the ground since newborns are considered divinities from heaven. While some parents, around the world, don't feel safe letting their babies play on the floor, as a method of preserving the child's health Bailanese babies cannot touch the ground until the 210th day of their life. That's amazing, we couldn't even have thought like that. Due to the fact that the baby is considered a divine being,who descended from heaven, when the child's feet touch the ground for the first time, it symbolizes that they have become fully human! What we can learn from this is that every child is divine, and must be treated right, in all elements and grounds of life. Why not give them a spa for 210 days? I think, parents can teach the child how to contact life joyfully at this time. Every moment feels so prayerful.

Trinidad: Put money in the baby's hand in order to bring prosperity to the newborn. In Trinidad and Tobago when people visit newborn babie they usually put money in the baby's hand in order to bring prosperity and good luck to the new born. Another custom from this country is that some parents do not allow people to come into their house after 6 p.m., since it is believed the evening dew will make the baby sick.

Brazil: The mother prepares souvenirs for each person who comes to visit the baby. (Brazil). In Brazil an expectant mother prepares baskets with souvenirs that are given to each person who comes to the hospital when the baby is born. Usually, the gift is something small such as candles, fridge magnets, customized notepads, magazines or tiny bottles of perfume, all of which are chosen by the mother before the baby is born.

Malaysia: Hot stone massages. A new Malay mother Undergoes a pantang, a confinement lasting about 44 days which is designed to preserve the health and femininity of the mother.She then receives hot stone massages to cleanse the womb and a full body exfoliation treatment which is said to smoothen and lighten the skin, and chase away postpartum changes. New moms are not allowed to lift heavy things or do anything apart from nursing the baby. All of the house chores fall onto the husband.

Source- "oddee.com"

Message to the reader

The lap of love and 'care'

Nurturing the baby why I called this chapter Lap of love and care because we have to learn as parents and individuals the balance between attachment and detachment also learning and welcoming our own inner child if we keep smothering or mothering our children, we have to look did we receive less that we believe we need to give so much here, can I give in a less smothering way? also helping clingy babies to become less clingy, and interdependent, me and the world, and helping the toddler grow from your lap into the welcoming world., where you have to learn to heavily let go of your baby, and also, learn a balance of over nurturing, or under nurturing, but return to balance nurturing and receiving, its about also relearning what you had forgotten as a parent or a wise child, this book overall is not only about wise parent but also the wise child in us as all is good if you begin to start learning again. I also give credits to brain rules for baby By John medina, and balanced and barefoot By Angela. We all have felt experienced being free of responsibility, and then tied or committed to them, that is the natural way to be in practical life, ideally it is good to have a balance, of work and play, responsibility and rejuvenation, right this chapter informed you about embracing your wonder of being or becoming a parent, its about finding your center and balance which we often lose or forget in modern life, due to modern lifestyle pressures, and if you have an interest in child development I am sure this chapter would have filled your mind with that whether you are going to be a parent, just curious, a learner this chapter must have informed you and enriched your mind to contribute in a more happier way.

Quote to ponder: Do you know that you carried you, before you carried the baby, you carried you so you could carry another life which you didn't know you would but you did, and if you did, do so with great fullness, no shame innocence, faith purity and love.

Get to know yourself all over again, let go of rigid rules of how you are supposed to be act and do.

Do you remember a time when everything worked out wonderfully without your much effort or desire to control the outcome?

P.s do you know I had to edit the book over 15-20 times to get it right?

(I didn't want it perfect, but I definitely had to work around a lot to get it flowing the right way!)

Sometimes we learn to be a parent the same way, that is why it is totally ok to be kind and gentle with yourself, and get enriched and grow in the process.

Notes

1. What were some of the favourite lines from this chapter.
How did it make you Feel?

_____

_____

_____

_____

_____

_____

_____

_____

_____

_____

2. What insights did you receive to make your experience more enriching and meaningful?

_____

_____

_____

_____

_____

_____

_____

_____

_____

Enriching Chapter 5

Embracing the empress in you
Effortless Bliss & Experience

Reflection moment

Appreciate the moment, stop and breathe be thankful for all you have and where you are today because this time next year or in 2 years, everything wont be the same there will be either added beauty joy or extra sorrow self pity or hatred we do choose all the way.

Its safe to receive love from my parents and from my own self. "Its safe to feel and be beautiful during my pregnancy, because mother earth wants me to feel her beauty and remind me of care and importance of caring for my inner and outer beauty."

"Its safe to feel truly secure, because father earth wants me to feel secure good enough, and Loved as I am." Its safe when I remember I am safe.

Throughout the previous chapter you read how to make a gentle and nurturing space for your baby, In this chapter you will read and learn how to prepare yourself physically in body and mind and learn more properly about your own body and mind, so you can be physically (body), emotionally (emotions) and psychologically, prepared for this important phase of your life, this chapter focuses totally on the pregnant Woman's body so delve deeper and explore the gifts of becoming a pregnant parent. (*The empress*) I have written on the empress, the connection with our feminine self, the process of writing this chapter was really wonderful as the information connected with each other quite beautifully, well but connecting with the empress that we are requires us to dwell and find confidence in our body in a deeper and a richer way, I developed my own health care and followed it, there were old emotions and stoppages I met from the past, which I had to embrace and bring home to love again, and that obviously just required me to remember that I am loved. As you will read below feel the lakshmi within you, these archetypes of gods and goddesses we see everyday, and we notice their qualities and learn to imbibe in our lives, our experience becomes so wonderful and value filled. Down below you will be informed about the trimesters, obviously the factual information is researched, my inutive sharing is a culimination of what I have learnt in my mind- body workshops and also what has worked for me to make peace with my body. I have to tell you I have not gotten sick in the past one year, or 2, and I am greatful this attitude is going to make me into a parent who can handle a baby.

This chapter is a friend of every growing woman, a homemaker and even the beautiful empress in us who has such beautiful colors. all of us are unique beautiful and special with our own unique qualities.

I remember our mother telling me when we were young, every girl is her own unique kind of flower, just shine and bloom gently and be the best self you can be.. never let your sense of self and experience be defined by only one role, you could be a caring sister, and a loving wife, and the most amazing parent, but if you don't accept yourself just the way you are, how will you notice the same in loved ones? or even your growing up children.

I let all roles of my life play our gracefully beautifuly and originally. The Empress shows a deep connection with our femininity. Femininity translates in many ways – beauty, sensuality, fertility, creative expression, nurturing – and is necessary in creating balance in both men and women. The Empress calls on you to connect with your feminine energy. Create beauty in your life. Get in touch with your sensuality through taste, touch, sound, smell and sight. Draw on these senses to experience pleasure and deep fulfilment. Treat yourself to a day spa, learn massage, enjoy a fine dining experience, or simply spend more time with your partner. Discover new ways to creatively express yourself, be it through painting, music, drama, or other art forms.

When we allow ourselves to truly experience the connections with Mother Earth, our femininity and those around us, we create abundunce and radiance in our lives. Take a moment to reflect on the love that surrounds you and build on this energy to create even more abundant love in your life. Know that love is limitless. A wonderful affirmation associated with the Empress is, "I bring forth my creations with joy, and I lovingly nurture them to fruition."

Where women are allowed to create, express themselves and be means their creative expression is honored. When it is honored, we must remember the royal and loyal treatment we deserve to give and receive in return.

Mantra

KaragrevasateLakshmi karamdhaye saraswati
Karmaddhye tuGovindah prabhate kardarshan

It means that Lakshmi rests a the tip of hand,Saraswati at the base of hand and Govind in the centre of hand.therefore one should look at the hand in the very morning.It conveys the following meaning, we do all our works by fingers of the hand to earn our livlihood.Therefore Lakshmi rests in the fingers which is tip of our hand.

Saraswati rests at the base of the hand.It means to say that all the books which are store houses of knowledge are held at the point where hand joins wrist ie base of hand whenever we open the books for study.

Govind rests at the middle of palm to signify that He keeps equal distance from wealth and knowledge. Also tips of our fingers come to the middle of palm at the same level when hand is closed to make fist. It means that men with different amount of wealth become of equal level when they get proximity of Govind.

Thus it has been impressed upon all to look at the palm in the very morning just after getting up. To allow in more harmon knolwedge and right and sensitive action.

Gentle writer and thinker.

- How to bring Lakshmi into your home and life
- Asthalakshmi the Eight lakshmis.
- **Adi Lakshmi**: The priveal Lakshmi.
- **Dhanalakshmi**: Money or gold. lakshmi
- **Dhyana Lakshmi.**: Goddess of grain, and giver of agricultural wealth.

- **Gaja Lakshmi**: Giver of animal wealth like cattle And elephants. according to Hindu mythology, GajaLakshmi brought back the wealth lost from the ocean.
- **Santana Lakshmi**: Giver of offspring.
- **Veera Lakshmi**: Courage to overcome difficulties in life.
- **Vijaya Lakshmi**: the one who brings victory.
- **Vidya Lakshmi**: bestower of knowledge arts and sciences.

A graceful empress has learnt from the depth of her emotions, what it means to truly give and receive blessings, and Grace.

Please find solutions for all these negative acts of society, and world so our children don't fall 'prey' to their actions because we don't deserve it allow it it wont happen. Please give us strength courage and esteem and honor to live in happiness and abundance.

So be it, it be so. And also let us remember the people who love us and hold it as the most precious gift. Because those who love us guard us protect us nurture us and nourish us in the best manner they know how. Betraying them would be like betraying the highest love and the truest prayer.

May there be peace in our culture may we evolve from being animalistic to angelic slowly but surely.

This little prayer was created after feeling deeply touched, by what people must go through with these negative acts.

Forgiveness

Every time we act unconsciously or with lack of seeking harmony in some way, well there is so much in the world to love, yet sometimes unconsciously we focus on pain, anger or separation, or we don't give space to our good memories, or let the good unfold for us, when we remember that we can face life than hide behind shadows, we find peace and even see glimpses of trust developing again, where there was only hatred now there is healing. That is a real shift. *Its natural to allow love in when we forgive.* We have forgiven when we finally feel restful and loving and believe we deserve good now, love now, when we change our perception our reality changes the acronym of forgive.

Rainbows are symbol of hope, gaze at the rainbow to life your spirits and renew your optimism.

- Freshness
- Offering
- Renewed
- Gratitude giving
- Intrest
- Very loving
- Exchange.

When we again look with love we know we have been forgiven, when the exchange in the moment is fresh, and it of love which can make us grow rather than be gripped in the ties of fear we have started to forgive.

Have you forgiven and given yourself another glorious chance to be more conscious? And caring and careful Forgiveness is already sitting with you!

Breathe in give good, Breathe out receive good, Replace that with a new Gift, A new habit, A new way to live, or a new way to relate and see stale situations (meaning of freshness).

These are some safe remedies to use in your pregnancy.

Aromatherapy	Accupressure	Ayurveda	Flower remedies
Primariliy refers to the healing through olfaction. Some aromatic essential oils, can also be ingested. And rubbed directly on the skin and Providing theraputic, benefits in the same way as other herbal medicines do. When inhaled, scents affect the limbic system of the brain the area associated with memory emotions and sexuality.	Activates the flow of the chi, by applying gentle pressure to the sensitive points, along the meredians. Instead of inserting, needles into them. This less invasive therapy, is good for people, who are squeamish, about needles and can be used as a self help procedure. Shaistu is a popular form, of accupressure.	Ayurveda which means, science of life which dates back, to 3000 BC, and is rooted in indian and hindu phillosphy. Ayurvedic medicine involves balancing a life force called prana. It considers the force of the wind. The tides and water and heat and the sun is significant factors,	Were initially developed by the english physician Edward, by placing flowers in a bowl of water, and setting them in sunlight, which allows their life forces and healing vibrations to influse, into the water. Each flower possess, specific, characterstics, that when the liquid is ingested, interact wth the persons,bodies, and calms their nerves. Bleeding heart for instace helps to cure the pain of a if ever broken heart, and impatience.
Heals the back the pressure points in body.	Heals the back, and hands, excellent for labor. During pregnancy you must avoid pressure points on lower back, sacrum and abdomen, but you can wear 'accupressure chappals at home' They will massage your feet as you will walk.	Good to imbibe In the dishes.	Excellent for insomnia (sleep problems) or others.

Reiki	Sound healing.	Journalling
Reiki actually means, universal life force, energy,	Proposes that each note of the musical scale corresponds in vibration to a particular, part of the body. Sound, waves are directed to the area where the healing is needed.	Journalling is a way to communicate with your mind and your innermost heart about your to do lists,next steps even how you feel about the enviorment and what your better trying to express or reveal to others or make a point and is not reaching.
Althought the term is used, interchangebly, with the practise of focusing, chi for emotional and physical healing.		
	Excellent for healing of the sensess	And you can also write letters, to your coming baby, you can write I love myself letters,
Excellent for better energetic and spiritual health during pregnancy.		Whats good about you,
Light rieki is recommended but intense as it can affect the baby.		You can either journal or say it out aloud, whatever you are comfortable with.
		Excellent to pen down your thoughts.

orange	red	yellow	green	blue	indigo	purple	pink
Orange represents warmth, orange has many meanings, including, warmth, sensuality, Peace.	The color red, is vibrant and full of life, and it means It also excites and energizes.	Yellow is a bright happy Joyful color!:) It means optimism Idealism and hope	Green is the color of the nature and environment Green is also the color of the Heart chakra	Blue holds the symbolic truth of Peace, Spirituality And truth	Indigo holds, the promise of knowing, and royalty, and even, privacy,	Purple is the color of, spirituality, and royalty again.	Pink is a soft color, and is usually carried off by the feminine.
Vibrations of the color orange. Amber, saffron, Apricot Coral.		Yellow is the color of the solar plexus chakra.	Green attracts attention for sure. Hence it's a nice color to carry on an important conversation.	Blue is the color, of Cool water And it represents Trust and harmony	Wearing it to formal occasions, really works well,	Wearing it to formal and informal occasions, attracts, Harmony and peace. And even spirituality.	Wearing pink, to Occassions, of birthdays and weddings and events, makes a really sweet statement.

Detoxing—

What is it?

A process or period of time in which one abstains from, or rids the body of, toxic or unhealthy substances; detoxification.

Detoxing is a process through which we let go of unhealthy substances, germs, and impurities that collect over the years from our body. Your body will begin to feel lighter, happier, healthier and more resistant to diseases which plague so many people. All you need to do is start!

How to detox at home

Cut out chemicals and toxins from your 'diet' include aloe vera juice and wheat grass shots and also include fresh juices. Inquire about colon cleanse which is available at 'detox centers' around the world and When you enroll in a detox program, you are totally focused on getting cleansed. There are many detox centers around the world. Just find one near you.

The practice of coloncleansing dates back to ancient Greece. In the U.S., cleansing the colon--the large intestine -- became popular in the early 1900's.

Is colon cleansing good for you?

Scientific research on colon cleansing is extremely limited. There is no good evidence for most of the claims that its practitioners make. And the side effects can range from mild to severe.

What is natural colon cleansing?

There are two main colon-cleansing methods. One involves buying products; the other involves seeing a practitioner to have a colon irrigation.

Although colon cleansing is not recommended during your pregnancy, you can do it before and after it,for pre-pregnancy and post-pregnancy health. Daily renewal renew yourself each day and do it again and again and again.

Hormones of pregnancy and labor, Estrogen and progesterone these hormones fluctuate throughout a womans menstrual cycle during pregnancy both hormone levels continue to rise, contributing to many physical and emotional changes, women experience. The sudden drop in these hormones after birth are associated with baby blues.

Oxytocin: This is called a love hormone, oxytocin plays a vital part in birth and breastfeeding as well as sexual pleasure, the release of oxytocin stimulates, contracts in childbirth and milk ejection in breastfeeding, this hormone is also associated with bonding. Pitocin, is the synthetic version of oxytocin typically used in induction of labor and augmentation.

Prolactin: This hormone is associated with the formation and production of milk. Stimulating the nipple and aerola and promotes the release of the hormone.

Endorphines: Reffered to as natures morphine, endorphins are responsible for the Euphoric feeling associated with immediate birth. The rise in oxytocin stimulates the release of endorphins and this interaction of hormones allows woman to challenges of labor.

Role of placenta in pregnancy: Placenta is the organ that develops your uterus during pregnancy, it transfers and provides Oxygen and nutrients the growing baby and removes toxins from your baby's blood

What is oxytocin?

Oxytocin helps in our emotional a well our physical transition to motherhood. From the first weeks of pregnancy, oxytocin helps to be more emotionally open and receptive to social contact and support, as the hormone of labor, orgasm, and breastfeeding.

You should know that levels of Oxytocin increase during labor and birth, they are the highest around birth. Hence for a woman to have a good relationship with her health, she should really learn to revere her health and body, and also be in gratitude like lakshmis lotus closes and opens, same way, the passage at birth opens like a lotus, and shuts off after birth. No matter how euphoric one can feel at a certain time, it is short lived but investing in good health is a long term investment.

Hormones- harmony / happiness of refreshing matters of new enrich sensuality / sexuality / surrender its so important to have a partner you can trust who gives you strength and encouragement as much as he or she is capable of being and giving during your pregnancy and also this reminds us to remind ourselves that only we are responsible for our own happiness, and well our biology controls our hormones and its natural but we can choose our feelings at the brightest level. Are my hormones in harmony or are they out of control?

Do you know without hormones we would feel no bubbling excitement to do anything? Hormones are responsible for sexual development, and even secreting of the happy oxytocin hormone and much more!

Dictionary definition of hormones

A regulatory substance produced in an organism and transported in tissue fluids such as blood or sap to stimulate specific cells or tissues into action.

- A synthetic substance with a similar effect to that of an animal or plant hormone.

- A person's sex hormones as held to influence behaviour or mood.

Psychological and social perspective which affect our biology. Imagine a woman doing the work of a man,and not finding time to be the woman that she is, that is sheer imbalance, when we stop finding joy in your own life and being your hormones get imbalanced true these are normal aspects of life, but you must face them. To understand your hormonal health, you have to understand your endocrine system. The endocrine system is responsible for coordinating the relationship between different organs and hormones, which are chemicals released into your bloodstream, within your endocrine glands.

What else imbalances the hormones?

What stops the harmony?

Dominating conversations: I don't want to hear you, I wont let you speak.

Over thinking: Why? Life is to experience it.

Over attachment with things and events and the way things could be: fear of now owning your own perception or creativity.

Cheating – lack of integrity.

Finding excuses – Ill exercise some other day, ill work some other day.

Spending too much time on social media- no real contact with freshness or life. Lack of faith in living.

Signs of hormonal imbalance

Weight gain or weight loss: its natural during pregnancy don natura just get enough sleep.

Loss of periods: Its natural

Depression: Think of good memories, through your life, clutter, clear, minimalize.

Practice: Heartfulness and mindfulness be responsive and responsible

Fatigue: Try walking on cold sand or using cold packs cool the sand in a fridge and walk on it, or touch it, it really balances and heals fatigue. Insomnia- use essential oils, be honest with your happiness levels.

Low libido: During pregnancy, it's natural to have low libido, however, channelize that energy into focusing on your heart and feeling joy, and practice **pre-natal yoga**, and practice cuddling and affection more.

Changes in appetite: Experiment and find joy in food rather than have to meal. Well, you have to take in all Vitamins, supplements and minerals, but be wise.

Digestive issues: Be honest about your stimulation, your intake and outtake through the day, don't overdo anything. Fear affects digestion, finding what you fear, and facing it is the key, and be honest.

Hair loss and hair thinning- apply oil. And get hair spas very often.

Being aware of 'Movements, and Hormones'

And what we see during pregnancy affects us well, the only balance you are meant to take care of is physical, sitting straight, being posture aware. It takes patience to cultivate that, its normal to lose your cool when you stop enjoying the process, hence, in order to bring in enjoyment and grace in your pregnancy, its important to balance your hormones, and to respect the smooth times of positivity, and then again deep rest, and little active stages, pregnancy consists of all of them. so what makes you truly happy? Happy hormones, make a healthier, and harmonious baby, so make it a priority, to nourish your hormones!.

Watch your movements keep a gentle watch at this. Shows how you are also feeling and how your baby must be feeling. The more graceful your movement is, the more gracefully your baby will perceive movement the more uneasy your movement is, your baby will feel it too, so be movement consious and effortlessly.

Resting should be a rejuvenating and important time of your schedule, so avoid watching Television, or use phones at all, this will keep you calm focused and in the moment, to what is Happening Now.

Dharmic Affirmation

I move with effortless ease into positive and nourishing experiences.

- By valuing your
- Freshness
- Joy
- Faith
- And rejuvenating your
- Peace
- Patience
- And process

You will experience and have more freshness joy and faith you are marrying your outer beauty beautifully and you can lead your beauty than be led by commercials and toxic beauty products which are harmful for the environment and you.

Taking care of your skin

Our skin is the largest organ of the body below are some skin problems that you should be aware of!

Abscess: A local infection which is painful, swollen and contains pus formation.

Acne: redness of the nose cheeks caused by dilation of the minute capalleries of the skin

Allergy: sensitivity causing the skin to react which becomes red hot and itchy

Spider naevus: small painless spot with thin blood vesseks that usually appear on the face body and legs during pregnancy.

Strech marks: thin lines of over stretched skin

Sunburn: inflammation of the skin after excessive exposure to the sun

Warts: small solid growth on skin caused by virus. Highly contagious.

The skin is the largest organ of the body, to protect and treat it beautifully means we are protecting the outer temple that covers our body.

Hair loss

Hair loss in women is a difficult diagnose and can be caused by many factors. Hormone imbalances effect of menopause shortage of dietry protein. Damage from hair treatments stress and shock after effect of fever effect of childbirth.

Keep in mind that hair loss can occur from the above but it can also occur from bad nutrition and stress, or sometimes even Heriditry affects hair loss, what you have to remember to keep in mind is that, it can be helped and below are some ways to help and prevent hair loss.

- I call it entangled.

- Improve your diet

- Don't collect stress or shock (means be aware of your emotional responses to life)

- Don't do activities you don't love.

- How to heal it using ointments from nature.

You can address and take care of your skin and hair even better when you are pregnant because fertility is your focus and you can invest in beautifully always go for products which are handmade and don't come in heavy or too many bottles less products means less worry more breathing space and beauty.

Avoid being tangled everywhere and protect your wisdom and respect your scalp. focus on scalp care, and get your head massages often!

Remember to have a sardarji day which means protecting your hair always when you move out in smoke and pollution and even sometimes having an indoor spa day.

Did you know?

Teratogenesis

Teratogenesis means the formation of the abnormalities in the baby during intrauterine life. The formation that leads to abnormalities are known as teratogens. Such abnormalities may be obvious when baby is born.

Lets explore the facts that lead to Tetratogenesis infections in the mother like, viral bacterial and fungal infections. Any micro organisms or the toxins released by them which cross the placenta and reach the baby might interfere with the development of the baby, and causing malformations.

For infections, maintain hygiene, wash your hands often, use of essential oils and remain in health full surroundings with clean bedsheets and frequent health checkups.

Addictions: drugs, Liqor, smoking and other addictions like Tabacco, chewing etc in the mother, these cross the placental barrier and might damage the baby. if the damage is intense it might lead to aboriton.

Physical violence, trauma, radiation from atom bombs, solar eclipse, can turn out to harmful for the mother and baby. Physical trauma can occur during journeys, sports like horse riding, trekking, mountaineering, gymnastics. You can walk but you cant do intense activities for sure. The industrial pollution is not likely to have noticeable effects. Naturally, stay inches away from these dangers. Vitamin and mineral deficiencies can also have in adequate or underdevelopment of the baby.

What is a toxin?

A poison of plant or animal origin, especially one produced by or derived from microorganisms and acting as an antigen in the body. We are used to living a toxic life without even realizing it, I remember when I went for my first detox, I realized how acidic my body was, well comparatively it wasn't so acidic because I usually follow an alkaline lifestyle, but it was acidic.

It is so important to get rid of these toxins we end up storing in our bodies, and rejuvenate ourselves once in a while do keep the below in Mind. Spend time in nature take care of your health. Smile more. And say No to what you don't want to be 'near or close to' there is no need to pretend when discerning whats a toxin and what is good for you its nature tells you so. Get medical check ups try to avoid eating out in rainy seasons.

Its only natural, I realized this later that all of nature whatever we call natural thrives on internal nourishment, external nourishment and Sleep and rest and 5-10 minute of graceful movement to feel well throughout the day when any of this gets imbalanced we cant thrive.

Health does not always come from medicine, it comes from peace of mind, peace in the heart, and soul, it comes from tapping into the power of our graceful selves.

Expternal nourishment is the nourishment we allow ourselves to receive from nature, our surroundings, and our Food as well. how we take care of our outer beauty whether we are aware of the dirt collecting around in our environment or where we work. Internal nourishment and nurturing is the diet we take in our food whether we are taking in minerals and vitamins from all food sources.

Beauty nourishing sleep means, are we letting our man and tan rest during sleep? if our mann does not sleep, so will our mind be busy. When our mann sleeps and so does our tann then when mann tann cooperate, we are headed to excellent nourishing gentle sleep! and we feel nourished relaxed and more alert during the day.

Beautiful movement people who live in natural areas and have less access to motion sickness can harness the beauty of movement. We can learn to move with grace simplicity again. When our movement carries that grace we will know. And we will have natural movement than controlled movement.

We need control movement when we are using a machine or something that requires our full body attention, but just a loving walk in your garden brings in the graceful movement. or doing a task with loving alertness.

How to avoid backache and swelling

Exercise often. Avoid heavy lifting and always bend your knees when lifting objects below your waist practise yoga, rest with feet elevated. Limit your salt intake. Relax in a warm aroma bath. Receive back massages and relax, and release tight muscles. Take time to rest. Apply warm heat to your back. Drink fluids. Sleep with pillows under your knees and use pillows to support your back and growing belly.

When to call your health care provider

It's important for you to stay in communication with your health care provider, the following are certain symptoms that should be brought to immediate attention of your health care provider— stay conscious of these symptoms, consult a doctor if needed, and seek natural remedies too.

Vaginal bleeding

Severe or persistent abdominal pain or cramping. Severe headache or blurred vision. Shortness of breath or chest pain. Swelling of your ankles. Reduced urine output. Burning or discomfort during urination. Fever of 101 degree Celsius. Fluid leaking from your vagina. A decrease in fetal movements. Marked gain in weight. An increase in pelvic pressure before 35 weeks of gestation.

How to combat fatigue

Rest, Rejuvenate and be in the moment, than living in a pricey future for which you have to sacrifice the simple joys of your present.

Activities forbidden during pregnancy

- Please avoid— Heavy weight training.
- Do not exercise lying on your stomach.
- Avoid using pesticides.
- Avoid using laptop on your lap.
- Amusement rides.
- Running and jogging.
- Cycling.
- High impact aerobics.
- Rigorous or labor work, ensure your heartbeat is 180 beats per minute.

- Downhill skiing or snowboarding.
- Scuba diving, surfing, or water skiing.
- Tennis.
- Horseback riding.

Tips for the pregnant mother:

When in 2nd trimester don't sleep on the back. it could restrict the amount of nutrients which could reach your baby. sleeping on your right is ok, not as good as sleeping on your Left. Try putting left leg up while sleeping. Sleepiing on your left hand side sends, nutrients and O2 more closely to the baby and Oxygen. Sleeping on your left, improves circulation. If you've been sleeping on your back all the time, till today its best to master your sleeping left position til your pregnancy. use gudied meditation, breathing excercises, before sleeping take often naps during the day Use your maternity pillow, available easily in the market these Days.

Where do you gulp with fear, with overwhelment or imbalance? Its time to talk to your partner. Don't keep gulping silence or fear, always communicate

What is hypertension?

Hypertension is an enemy of your wellbeing during pregnancy.

What is hypertension?

Hypertension is high blood pressure in which the force of your artery walls is high enough, that it may eventually cause health problems. Normal blood pressure Is between 100-140 mm high blood pressure goes up to 144.90.

Hypertension classified as either primary hypertension which means high blood pressure with no possible medical cause, where as the remaining are caused by other conditions that affect the kidney arteries heart or endocrine system.

What causes hypertension?

No exposure to natural light, too much indoors less fresh air, chemicals inhaling in the enviroment in activity. High salt intake digestion problems. tobacco being over weight or obese too much salt or alcohol. stress illegal drugs sedantary lifestyle.

Uncontrolled high blood pressure can lead to almost all minor and major tension/ blood/ heart diseases are caused by the above. Heart attack or stroke. Heart failure.

Weakened or narrowed blood vessel and kidneys. (this prevents these organs from functioning normally.

How to keep hypertension or heart attack inches away?

- Eat healthy foods.
- Decrease the salt in your diet.
- Maintain a healthy weight
- Get enough sleep.
- Increase physical activity
- Don't smoke
- Limit alcohol.
- Keep environment fresh and clean.

- Water your plants
- Sit in sunlight.

Also we are tensed because, we are anxious about the future and don't like the present or simply have less interest at the moment, take it as a sign to rest holiday or rejuvenation.

Graceful Affirmation

I keep hypertension inches away realizing that anytime I am not happy, I am less aware and conscious of what is happening and where I am going and its ok, I am human.

A disease can spread, but one good habit can help heal the unease caused by Dis-eases. The body and mind are connected, this means that what affects the body comes from the mind and what affect the mind becomes from the body. To keep both of them healthy and happy is an ideal state we all crave for, and it is possible, just with a little awareness and remembering this, we can keep certain diseases and problems at bay, yoga teaches us this, and so many other phillosophical teachings.

Affirmation

I am in harmony with my blood pressure.
I notice when I am getting blind to my own true self and its progress.
I am in harmony with what my heart wants.

Nervous problems arise from nerves are the receptors of our body when we aren't communicating clearly or disagreeing with something someone for way too long or our creative or nervous energy is not channeled correctly, we face nervous problems and breakdowns and these are not friends with a happy experience of pregnancy so if you have nervous problems or have had them before, find out,If you Are too self centered or take your receptivity and sensitivity for granted. This means what you truly want to do and say think hear and experience are out of harmony hence to harmonize this,take care of your words and actions and believe in a higher power.

According to louise Hay who is the Authoress of All is well, and other books says: the nervousness problems omes from anxiety, and not trusting the process of life.

Home for the empress

Paying attention to your kitchen.

Build appetites in your kitchen with red: **Red** and you can also use **Green**, however it is said that keeping natural stones in your kitchen can make your kitchen more harmonious, it is about making your kitchen feel creative, and positive as much as you can. However **red** has been shown to increase appetite in most people one of the reasons that many restaurants choose red patterns in their dining rooms. Using **red** in your kitchen to increase appetite is as simple as blending beige walls with red shutters or cabinet doors. also try, to use more natural and organic material in your kitchen which improve your life quality and eating quality. The kitchen affects the rest of the house because everyone is looking forward to the kitchen morning evening and night. It will have a lot of storage, and there will be sharp items for sharp items, try to make a safe area where children cannot reach, a happy healthy kitchen has a loving quality. if one really pay attention you can add plants, and natural stones anything that reminds you of how precious sharing can be.

What can be an ideal position for the kitchen?

- The ideal position for the kitchen is on either the southern or eastern side of a house. It's also okay to have your kitchen positioned on the north, northeast, or southwest side. A kitchen in the southeastern corner is also a good direction for Feng shui since it represents the wood element, which can be a good source of energy.

- It is better to keep the kitchen separate from the dining room. It also shouldn't be below a toilet or adjacent to one.

- It is unfavorable to have it in the center of a home.

- The room shouldn't face the front door back doors or staircase, bathroom, or an adjoining room as such a placement encourages bad health, arguments among family members, and overall bad luck.

- Keep the kitchen door and any other doors closed as much as possible.

- **Fengshui fix:** If the kitchen is visible from the main entrance, put up a screen or beaded curtain.

- Placing Malachite, Chrysoprase, and Moss Agate crystals in the kitchen is also a good idea.

Affirmation

Our kitchen is happy holistic kind and trustworthy energy
and gives of positive fengshui, because it is a place of creativity care and cooking.

- In pregnancy you will use the bathroom a lot in fact because of so many symptoms of pregnancy require the washroom, however keep it positive by placing a plant there and keep it fragrant as much as you can, make sure it inspires relaxation and freshness.

Affirmation

Bathroom is a kind to my needs.
I live a life that requires me to let go more of what
is not good for me, and imbibe more beauty from the world.
So I have to let go of less and have what I truly need.

Mantra page

'Body tujhe salaam' body I appreciate you wholly.

Mantras for amore positive pregnancy

"My body is a vessel" — Helpful for women experiencing bodily discomfort or those who are uncomfortable with their changing shape and weight.

"My pregnant body is beautiful" –I accept and love my body just as it is.

"I am nourishing my baby's body'" — Helps to encourage choosing nutritious food and drink.

"I won't be pregnant forever" — Helpful for the end of pregnancy or for a pregnancy that is causing physical discomfort.

"My body is strong enough" — Helpful to overcome thoughts like, "I don't think I can do this!"

"This work is important, and essential" — Reminding yourself of your goal. I enjoy the glow of my pregnancy and include freshness in my perspective, feeling, and sharing.

"I listen to what my body needs" — Helps to respond better to cues of tiredness, hunger, needing time alone.

"One day/moment at a time" — Reminds you to only worry or focus on today.

"I am here for my baby" — Helps to connect you with your baby.

"My body is the perfect home for my baby" — Encourages you to trust your body and its ability to grow your baby.

"I make the best decisions for my baby and me" — Combats negative self-talk and unwanted advice from others

What are Limiting messages?

Limiting messages are messages with messages that we have stored inside, that are blocking or restricting our true potentional that we are capable of, at a certain time.

Every time you think about childbirth, what do you envision?

Some people envision 'too much stress' nervousness, morning sickness, you will experience what you believe, if you want it to be a happy balanced process you envision that, obviously to find real balance takes daily communication, and balance of our physical mental and emotional and even spiritual sides' every experience is fresh and unique, henceforth judgement shouldn't take a seat in this journey!

1ˢᵗ trimester

At about 14 days after an egg is released, combines with sperm and and conception occurs, there after a baby has started its graceful developing in 1ˢᵗ trimester.

The fetus begins to develop a brain and spinal cord. And the organs develop to form. The baby's heart will also begin to beat in the 1st trimester. You can hear your baby's heartbeat in this trimester.

What to do this trimester?

- Eat iron rich foods.
- Keep yourself lightly active
- Follow a balanced lifestyle.
- Create a balanced diet chart
- Avoid heavy junks
- Eat all tastes in moderation.

2ndtrimester

The beginning of the third trimester babies are about, 3.1/2 inches long, and weigh about 1/1/2 ounces. Their tiny unique fingerprints are now visible, the heart pumps, 25 quartz of blood a day. As these weeks go by your babys skeleton starts to harden from a rubbery cartilage to bone. One is likely to feel flutters and kicks more often in this trimester. You can hear your babies, heart beat this trimester.

What to do this trimester?

This is a trimester when you will need gentle movement, A lot of rest, So avoid stimulation in excuse, Again follow a balanced and a kind approach.

3rdtrimester

Babies weight around 2/1/4 pounds by the start of the third trimester. They can blink their eyes, which now sport lashes, and their skin starts getting wrinkly, they are also developing fingernails, toenails and real hair, and adding billions of neurons into their brain, your blossoming baby will spend his or her weeks in utero putting on weight. At full term, the average baby is more than 19 inches long and weighs nearly 7 pounds. The baby is getting prepared to come out and is mostly developed.

This trimester is when the baby is ready to come out, eat balanced foods and consume healthy calcium, iron, protein in small quantities keep yourself fresh and ready for the delivery by practicing pre natal yoga, learning labor techniques and staying bright.

Painting by Jai Ranjit, Mumbai

A prayer for peace of soul during Pregnancy.

Go placidly amid the noise and haste,
Take kindly the counsel of others and years,
Gracefully surrendering the things of youth,
Nurture strength of spirit, to shield you in
sudden misfortune.
But do not distress yourself, with imaginings.
Many fears are born out of fatigue and
lonliness. Beyond a
Wholesome discipline, be gentle with yourself.
You are a child of the universe, no less than the
trees and the stars, you have a
Right to be here, and whether or not it is clear
to you darling,
No doubt the universe is unfolding as it should.
Therefore be peace with god
Whatever you conceive him to be,
And whatever your labors, and aspirations in
the noisy confusion of life,
Keep peace with your soul,
With all the wisdom, drudgery, and
broken dreams
Its still a beautiful world.
Be careful, yet strive to be happy.
Found in old saints church, Baltimore.
Acknowledge the shift in yourself and others,
with appreciation, friendship and Joy.
That is also the gift of peace and togetherness

Weight gain

We all know a well-balanced nutritional program generally leads to a healthy and bigger babies. In general, a weight gain of 25 to 35 pounds leads to the healthiest newborns. These extra pounds are composed of the following:

- Baby- 7 1/2 pounds.
- Uterus-2 1/2 pounds
- Placenta- 1 pound.
- Amniotic fluid- 2 pounds.
- Mothers breasts- 3-pound increase.
- Mothers blood- 4 pounds increase.
- Mothers fat- 5-pound increase.
- The total weight gain is usually 25 pounds.

A healthy nursing routine:
- Breast massage- Fennel with olive oil
- Thanking a fruit or a tree
- Milk thistle tablet.
- Fennel seeds.
- Use chemical free soap for better breastfeeding.
- Fenugreek powder with water.

Swelling during pregnancy

During pregnancy the body produces approximately 50 percent more blood and body fluids to meet the needs of the developing baby.

Swelling is a normal part of pregnancy that is caused by additional blood and fluid in areas like hands, face, legs, ankles, feet.

Causes

Growing uterus puts pressure on pelvic veins and vena cava, the pressure slows down circulation and causes blood to pool in the legs, being forced from veins into the tissues and legs.

Risk factors

- Summer time heat.
- Diet low in potassium.
- High level of caffeine.
- High or lowblood pressure.
- Medications.

Management

- Lie on the side.
- Get a massage.
- Try ice therapy.
- Try cold sand therapy.
- Take aromatherapy.
- Stretch legs frequently while sitting.
- Ankle toe movements.
- Take breaks from sitting/standing.
- Take a short walk often.

- Avoid tight clothing.
- Exercise like swimming can help you a lot.

To avoid and help vomiting, do move the limbs for a few minutes before getting out of bed. Avoid too much fried, fatty, or spiced foods. Avoid warm places since heat can create nausea feelings. Get out of bed slowly in the morning a meal. Avoid dehydration, drink small amount of liquids many time during the day. Drinking tea like ginger or peppermint Tea cure nausea. Good sleep and rest. Good sleep and even getting a massage can help with swelling.

Dealing with postpartum weight:

Here are some ways you can start losing weight. It's important to be fit for birth and afterbirth! Don't you think mommy?

- **Honey, lemon juice and black** pepper (do this daily for 3 months or more) This is healthy, light, and helpful for weight loss.

  1) **Apple cider vinegar-** You can have two spoons of apple cider vinegar per day, or mix it with your water.
  2) **Aloe Vera-** Aloe Vera reduces accumulation of body fat.
  3) **Green tea-** Green tea promotes weight loss.
  4) **Cayenne pepper-** Cayenne pepper is an antioxidant which supports during weight loss.
  5) **Curry leaves-** Curry leaves reduce body gain and increase your vitality.

Affection

Affection is truest form of expressing our love and close ness and fondness to someone. We deserve our own love and affection as lord Buddha said, affections language is free of judgement pain anger hatred or disbelief you can recognize a child who pushes away affection pushes away love in some form and naturally that child is learning to allow love. So help and heal yourself quickly with the dose and care of affection. So are you forgetting your own language of personal affection and letting it get overpowered by a the language to fit in or fear? Are you selling your precious time and attention too freely to get approval that really does not nourish your own soul, then you are betraying your heart, to save yourself from the language to be someone others want you to be, fill your life with affection, protection, nourishment, honor self love and care.

We all have done that, we forget the hours our parents truly give to make us feel secure, do you remember your first birthday? How lovingly the parents made efforts to invite your friends and make it special for you, do you remember the kind of expensive cakes and food that was ordered for you, well these things in life are for free, but so many people yet die of hunger and never having any one do that for them.

I realized that to honor 'this particular attribute is what I always want to keep on top of my priority list, to never forget my own language of affection and love and know that until my Cup is not full, its useless to give or pour it To anyone else.

What fills our cup of growing with wisdom and joy everyday?

Trust, faith, love, honest and maintaining my passion for living the happiest and brightest I can live. There will be dark times but they aren't there to pull me down but To empower me to even come out stronger. I fill my cup everyday before pouring it on to someone else whether it is cup of blessing Affection, Love, Friendship or care this way I am seldom drained and I can rise above Negativity quickly and not let it become part of my beautiful process of pregnancy.

All the previous information were coming from the belief that I can write, I can inspire, I can be like the empress, there is lack of self love and belief and acceptance that comes when we accept our beautiful unique selves just the way we are, without cutting out the flaws but even embracing the flaws, by getting to know oneself better we compromise with care, and consideration towards our self love and we don't harm life each other or ourselves. If you can love yourself you will love others. If you are a person who can read and see, I am also going to be making a audio cd of the main points for any workshops I do in the future, but if I do any workshop it will definitely be on self love acceptance and care. So read further on, and find these little nuggets and wisdom and flowers come into your being in the form of self love.

And also not to find fault with our shape size during pregnancy, those are illusions of beauty magazines that have actually no true description or what beauty truly is. And to also know when to put appropriate boundries if needed.

Our gods have much to teach us, here we aren't just worshipping god but actually inviting Divine into our lives and events and everyday life.

Finding strength and perfection in daily imperfection'

Ganesha or lakshmi learns form from the environment.
Its important to love our shape,
Our size,
Our curves
And our mistakes
Our pain,
Our faith
Our pleasure,
And our imperfect,
Weight gain,
Its negative to
Try to be perfect
To please, any
Race,
So why be judgmental to ourselves,
To our face,
Through the beautiful process of adding more weight?
What do u want your child to learn, from the environment when he comes?
Or, about food?
Choose, how you allow yourself, to be treated, and even treat others.
Since Ganesha and Lakshmi are learning through you,

About treatment, and being treated.
Beauty and expressing.
I create grace and Peace in little moments in my Day and Evenings.

Basic hygiene

Even in pregnancy the expectant mother should take care of her own physical hygiene. During pregnancy the vaginal discharge is on the rise, hence it is essential to keep private parts healthy and clean It is recommended to do a perennial massage, or to keep vagina lightly lubricated with healthy oils, since there is lot of vaginal discharge, the oil will keep it nourished.

TIP: A healthy pregnancy and a lifestyle requires us to manage our physical, emotional and mental hygiene'

Travel/ kaha-Jaye?

Long distance travelling should be avoided during the first three months and the last three months. One can travel in the second trimester (break and rest trimester). A refreshing holiday will do good at this time after consulting the doctor. It is advisable not to travel from 7th month.

What to listen to?/Kya-sune?

The mother can listen to calming and cheerful music, like flute, trumpet, Shehnai, Bhajans, nature sounds, whatever suits her and makes her feel good and releases the oxytocin from the brain, recitals of shlokas, and spiritual material is also healing during this time, If she has an interest in spiritual development.

What to read kya padhe?

Obviously read all nurturing material, and don't read violent or disturbing stuff, for a list of books you can refer at the back of the page'. Obviously choose, pleasant material to read, and not non violent, which would stress your nerves, and you can refer to back of the book for recommended reading page' which means do not read harsh violent material that would stress your nerves.

What to avoid listening to much

Pop music, harsh voices, rock music and sounds that induce violence and aggression, gossip should also be avoided.

Stories novels that can read but in limits, only if you can handle the difficult stories and can digest, anything that stresses the body mind and nervous system to put a lot of energy into the activity should be avoided, as the nervous system is busy supporting the baby's body at this time and any activity which takes away your attention from that act of creative loving kind gentle intelligence into anything harsh spoils the natures beauty harmony and grace. So avoid stuff that you may need to put a lot of nervous and pure attention to especially if its not worth your heart attention, be attention smart focus on one activity at a time, and be thick skinned, not light skinned or brained that anything can steal your attention, during pregnancy you have to maintain that harmony as much as you can like goddess Shakti's energy, or Radha's devotion, or Lakshmi's dignity, don't have scattered attention, be present as lovingly and willingly as you can. Imagine your attention is as priceless as Lakshmis attention, now will you sell that attention so easily? Avoid texting, chatting try to maintain a beautiful natural connection with earth.

What to see? Kya dekhe?

Natures beauty, trees, birds, fragrant flowers, and see what truly calls your heart, being the moment, and let things happen as they are happening faces of loved ones, Loving art, birds, laughter, singing children all recommended to see. And hear at this time. Just be natural, don't go the unnatural way.

What not to think? Kya soche?

The mother should not worry about her delivery or about her health, or finances, these areas should be managed before the decision to become pregnant. Emotions like these can stop the motion of a joyful 'pregnancy. Well it will take your effort but keep it simple.

Write a love and welcoming letter to the baby in your womb, and frame it somewhere, just go with your feeling and write. You can write my dear one, or you can think of a name just be intuitive.

Every individual is made in the image love likeliness and wisdom of Divine.
That is why comparison is so 'old thought'

And we are all so unique,
Isnt it a enchanting and a wise world?

The wonder of the uterus

- These are some amazing facts about the womb (uterus). The organ in the lower body of a woman or female mammal where offspring are conceived and in which they gestate before birth; the womb.
- Here is a little bit about our wondrous uterus(womb)
- The PH levels of the uterus is different from the rest of the body. It is very acidic, it's healthy acidic, it keeps bacteria and bugs away from the uterus. It's

actually quite healthy to keep bacteria and other bugs away, isn't it?

- Period protection has come a long way.
- Today, women keep menstrual blood at bay with pads, tampons and menstrual cups or even hormones that shut down the period all together. Women of the past had to be more creative.
- Softened papyrus (ancient Egypt)
- Lint wrapper around wood (ancient Greece)
- Paper (ancient Japan)
- Cellulose bandages (France, early 1900's)
- Menstrual blood is rich in stem cells which have been found to be adaptive within the body to heal a variety of diseases.
- The uterus can grow a baby.
- The uterus can grow a placenta.
- The uterus is the only organ that can grow a whole new organ within it! The placenta is absolutely amazing. It is responsible for transferring nutrients that nourish and maintain the fetus through the umbilical cord. The main cord is the main link from the fetus to the placenta. Through it the placenta provides O2 and nutrients to a growing baby, and removes waste products.
- Your uterus is nurturing the fertilized ovum that develops into the fetus, and holding it till the baby is mature enough for birth. The fertilized ovum gets implanted into the endometrium and derives nourishment from blood vessels which develop exclusively for this purpose.

- 11 healthy foods for a happy uterus.

- Flaxseeds.
- Olives
- Fiber rich foods.
- Fruits
- Lemon
- Fish
- Pomegranate
- Nuts
- Green leafy vegetables.
- Castor oil
- Berries.
- Pumpkin oil.

How to feel, Secure, peaceful allowing caring and embracing in a particular space. Every space has a different vibration a temples vibration cannot match a small corner or a storage room. A personal temple vibration cannot match a temple where people visit everyday. A schools vibration cannot mix with the feeling of a discotheque, Well it is that way, and to interfere with the natural order of things would be stupidity. Because what we do in a hospital we cannot do in a school, and what we do in a school, we don't do in big large temples.

Intention- *I respect the vibration of every place as it is, and find something good to add in there'.*

Sacred sweet space

Soulful, surrendering, wise, embracing, truthful Space.

Secure, peaceful, allowing, caring, embracing.
We choose whom we allow around the sweet
space we create around us,
That sweet space filled with sacred becoming of
who we really are, is meant to be
treasured and cared and loved by the person
We all share a relation with Our space
keep only forms of love in that space,
The space between the baby and the mother is
only such a small distance,
How long are we willing to go through
that space?
and bring in sweetness, and purity through,
it means we remember why we
stepped into that
space in the first place.
That is sweet space,
And no one is allowed to enter without your
permission. you are the gatekeeper, nurturer
and protecter of your sweet space.
You cannot master the rest of your life in one
day, master one day and keep doing that
every day.
Its safe to retreat into my sacred sweet space
That is remembering to wear your halo of
healing, allowing love of soul.

Written on january 2015

Touch of gentle care

This time is special so you need to arrange it accordingly
don't totally seclude the baby from the rest of the day for
this time but prepare the baby to receive gentle energy

and love during this time. Your little one is attuned to your emotions so be gentle and calm before starting take a sweet moment to let go of worries and concerns arrange a quiet sweet space for your massage time, overhead lights can be irritating For your baby, So turn on the small lamp instead. The room should be warm and not drafty. Turn off the telephone, have a blanket pillow oil and an extra diaper.

This is the time when you don't want to use phones, or get disturbed switch on your best loving gentle music, and start the massage. You can only massage when the baby is well if your baby is unwell as the doctor before starting the massage.

Do not massage your baby, if he or she is sick or has fever. Wait until the temperature are normal. Massage is not the replacement for medical attention by any means. You can start massaging a healthy baby soon after birth.

Touch is powerful and has been scientifically shown to have remarkable effects. It benefits both babies and parents by mutually reducing stress levels, improving communication, and strengthening and developing parent child bond. Touch helps infant to relax and develop better sleep patterns. It relives digestive comfort and is crucial for growth and development. It can create a solid foundation of trust joy and play with the parent. As the child grows.

As the child grows and develops the areas that they like to have massaged the most may change. For instance when a child starts to walk, he may prefer to have massage on the legs and back as they are holding baby up for the first time. You can use the same baby massage strokes for the older child. You will feel their muscles developing and strengthening under touch. Massage can help with growing pains anxiety even carrying back packs!

Your massage will gently get firmer and stronger, and do wait for the day when your child says *Can I give you a massage?*

Some tips about massage

Your touch needs to be gentle since the new borns bones are very soft. Your touch also needs to be firm so practise gentle strength. Changing positions while massaging them, such as on their side, on their tummy, on their back, or nestled close to you, helps their bodies strengthen in different ways. it takes many years before the childs nervous system matures, and in infancy they are very sensitive to enviromental stimuli, and need regular breaks, from it to rest. Be careful not to massage your baby after eating, it can interfere with her/his digestion. Begin at the center of the forehead, as it is very soothing.

When to massage the baby?

Suggested time to introduce baby to the loving art of massage are when your baby has just woken up from several hours of sleep. Has just had a bath and is feeling relaxed and happy. Or in the hour before bedtime. However the best time to begin is quiet alert time, which is newborns cycle that you sometimes swear your always active baby does not have. It does exist. And you can share you Sweet space nurturing touch massage sessions together.

On infant massage

Good oils to consider are coconut, olive and grapeseed massaging without oil has its own benefits, but it is dry and not smooth, maybe you can use oil in one massage and then in the other just use light feather touch and dry massage. Stay away from petroleum based products, because of possible allergens. Before using the oil, do place a drop on the outside of their upper arm or leg, first then wait for an hour. If the area doesn't turn red, your good to go and it is a good oil.

Oils good for your baby's massage

- Coconut oil
- Seaseme oil
- Mustard oil
- Olive oil

Sharing two techniques

The first leg stroke: behind the leg massage at the thighs with long downward strokes that encourage the muscles to relax. One hand will gently hold the ankle and foot and the other is cupped and follows the contour of the leg. This is also called Indian milking stoke. As it comes from the traditional Indian art of baby massage. Your touch is gently but firm, with long flowing strokes using as much of your hand as you can.

Your stroking hand is shaped like a C to conform the leg. Relax the weight by stroking hand so that it is gentle. But entire weight repeat this 'stroke' a few times, alternating hands like one wave following another.

Whatever our age when we receive a massage we let our guard down we become vulnerable, it is an intimate experience, we need to feel safe to trust the process, of massage and so do babies. Baby massage is about healthy respectful touch. Never end the massage abruptly bring the massage time to a gentle, if prompt close,winding down with a cozy graceful conclusion. After the last massage stroke and some gentle baby holds, make sure the baby is warm and close. Perhaps wrap her in a blanket the way she likes best. Some babies need their arms and hands free. Or simply hold him/ her.

You can add some music, chanting sounds, so you can hum, sing a lullaby, or put on relaxing Cd, Maintain the lovely connection and closeness as you both absorb the Experience. Ease your way back into the day together.

Nurturing affirmation: I massage our baby with tenderless , love and gentleness.

Caring touch

Touch your knees and thank it for acting as a connective tissue which connects your calves and your thighs, the lower and upper, Touch your heart and thank the organ for beating so beautiful, without your command to it, to beat it, right it's natures gift. Thank your eyes for blinking today. Touch your hands and tell them, thank you for moulding shaping, guiding, pointing, during your day. Touch your breast and tell it, thank you for being so cooperative and look forward to what and where you want to go. And do. And being so soft and caring. Touch your head and say thank you for being so obedient, for looking in any direction you wanted to look. Touch your back of the neck, and tell it thank you, for being straight and cooperating with my head and heart to achieve my day. Touch your back and tell it, thank you for being such a thick support to create a comfortable day for me. Touch your glands, organs, and nerves and tell them thank you for working so hard and so effortlessly and beautifully. Well, your organs work harder when your pregnant.

Being honest and Real about your 'capacity' to give, helps you deal with life's stresses better, there is no need to lie about how much you can Give' that is Love.

The feeling our soul is 'part of ' our daily activities and what truly matters to us is a feeling and note of joy and gladness to be alive.

Say goodbye to worry and embrace wisdom. Say goodbye to anger and embrace love. Say goodbye to doing things in one way, and embrace creativity. Say goodbye to greed and hello to gratitude. Read about the soul. Be like your soul.

The soul can be closely known through meditation, learning, healing practices, and living a balanced life. And being happy, you find your method during pregnancy that's more than enough at the right time. And trust in a higher power. Why do we go to temples, churches, and sacred places anyway?

To trust the higher power. Have a positive relationship with it. And your soul just knows 'how'.Just embrace qualities of it everyday in your life and it will reveal itself to you through small things that will delight, you surprise you, engage you, align you, teach you, and bring you grace, gratitude, and wisdom.

Mantra for security, stability, awareness, inner strength, and freedom from disease. Muladharabija seed sound Lang. VangshangKshang sang.

Activity

Preventions

Here are some ways you can prevent miscarriage:

Meet your gynecologist, first trimester, and in the middle, have a good relationship with them. Eat a well-balanced diet. exercise in moderation avoid drugs, smoking, or alcohol. Keep a clean and healthy mouth and gut.

If you have mild to severe back pain (which could mean you are taking more load than necessary, let go of fear, of anything, labor pains, just enjoy, let go centered in your being. Practice Kegel. Balance your hormones naturally.

- 15 tips for a healthy uterus and body image for women.
- In China they call a womans womb her inner palace, because it is a place to create for a future generation the next sons and daughters.
- Menstrual disharmonies such as painful periods.
- Uterine bleeding and infertility can be avoided and healed by taking better care of the womb.
- Avoid having too many sexual partners.
- Eat plenty of cold water fish, which is rich in omega 3.
- Eat less and balanced.

- Exercise your pelvic muscles, for example, do Kegels.
- Avoid using birth control pills.
- Maintain a healthy body weight.
- Keep your uterus warm.
- have a nutritious breakfast with some wholegrains.
- Pay attention to your vaginal discharge.
- Start drinking a cup of lemon water in the morning.
- Appreciate the divine intelligence of your body!

How to keep knee pain at bay

During pregnancy, there are many changes that occur in your body. Due to these normal changes,it is common to experience increased joint and muscle pain. Increased weight puts pressure on the knees, the connector tissue, and hence, you might have to pay attention to the knees.

Give 'I love you' knee treatment to knees every night before sleeping. Use cold pack. Do streches we do this when we sit in an upright position, We want to lie down but we pressurize ourselves to sit. Gently move into ideal position.

Get to know yourself Enrichy and blissfully

Insight through drawing

drawing and art is one way of expressing and expressing your feelings can be a way to access your gentle inner self, pictures can bypass verbal language to reveal the realm of your creative imagination, and give you new insight about your pregnancy and unborn baby. Give yourself permission to not be perfect, relax and unwind, and color your way through, release your inner critic and let yourself play, get a journal to write or draw in.

Tip: keep a journal

Make a happy sensation List. If you get sad or depressed, touch of cold water, smell of something nice, don't overcloud your aura with electronics, Appreciate your inner and outer beauty Inner beauty is what you cant see but beams through your eyes, your smile and your gestures.

Pray to a plant, Just stand near the plant and pray with it or near it, You will feel a sense of regaining your sensitivity.

The body of a woman who is to conceive is being chosen as a channel for the expression of divinity into materialization, although evolution is a law of nature, Conception is a law of the divine.

Enliven through your attention:

Mantagiyantra
For increasing abilities in speech music and creativity.

Aum Hringkling Hum

Mantagaiyephatswaha.

From the millions of cells interacting in our
bodies, it's all amazing tastes available to us,
pondering our total
interdependence on water, sunlight, trees that
grow in the earth, true wealth is the capacity,
to be constantly amazed and
grateful for everyday wonders of everyday life
If the Buddha had kids

The weeks story

12 weeks

Most women have their ultra sound by now.

13 weeks.

The pregnancy may not yet be visible on the outside
although most pregnant women have by now become a
bit wider. In the waist and around the hips. pregnancy
symptoms that you may be experiencing could include
fatigue headaches and nasal congestions. Increased saliva,
tender breasts and nausea and possibly faintness.

13 weeks and one day.

An amniocentesis test can be taken around a week in 16.
A thin needle is used to take some amniotic fluid via the
abdominal wall.

13 weeks and four days.

The baby can now bend his arms At the elbows and the
wrist, the fingers can bend and make a fist. The features
on the face the nose chin, and forehead Are becoming

more defined. Your baby may be trying out lip movements in preparation for reflex sucking action. The Foetus is now about 8.5 cm long.

14 weeks and 4 day.

The taste organs are now developing, the feotus recognizes the taste of amniotic fluid it is and take it in, partly through the skin and partly by swallowing it. Hair Is growing not only on the baby's head but also on the eyebrows and even eye lashes. The baby starts to lose her top heavy look as her overall height increases the legs are now longer than the arms. Baby is 11 cm/ in length

15 weeks and 1 day.

At birth your babys eyesight may be a little blurred. But he can focus on objects, held about 20 cm he will particularly be fascinated by objects that move, and there is a good chance, he can make out colours, babies are also born with several reflex actions, but blinking is the only one that they will keep for life.

16 weeks and four days

Your babys skin is becoming thicker.

17 weeks.

Most women who are experiencing their first pregnancy, regularly have short period of being Terror stricken. Luckily it will be an immensely rewarding journey. Once your baby has arrived.

10 days to go.

Babys development In these last weeks the baby is merely building their inner strength putting on weight and growin

"The peace of **God** is with them whose mind and soul are in harmony, who are free from desire and wrath, who know their own soul." "Perform all thy actions with mind concentrated on the Divine, renouncing attachment and looking upon success and failure with an equal eye.

'The solution to addictive behavior is to find a creative habit or talent that becomes more important than this painful addiction'

Quit your addictions

Smoking, drinking, over working, over thinking, anything that blocks that goodness in your body, mind, and soul is an addiction.

Addictions are filled with aggressions. I don't care I want to do it because It doesntmatter (I don't matter) you dontmatter life doesnt.

Life is important and so am I and so are my desires. My healing is other people's joy in my life. It benefits them and me.

We are in pain because we are going against the heart or the soul's wish, or allowance, that is why we suffer, anything that your heart says no to, you should stand by its side. Whose side are you on?

What is postpartum depression?

Postpartum depression may be mistaken for baby blues at first — but the signs and symptoms are more intense and last longer, eventually interfering with your ability to care for your baby and handle other daily tasks. Symptoms usually develop within the first few weeks after giving birth, but may begin later — up to six months after birth.

Postpartum depression symptoms may include:

- **Depressed mood** or severe mood swings- these are normal, but should not become so intolerable that it turns into depression, learn to identify where your mood is guiding you.

- **Excessive crying:** tHese ideally should be happy tears,unless they are not, and hence its so important to know what you are getting into and being conscious, but crying sometimes can prove healing, if it is done with someone you trust and you feel safe'.

- **Difficulty bonding with your baby**- Did you LOVE yourself as a baby? Did you truly bond with yourself? What do you like? What's your lifestyle preference, what DON'T you like? Whenever we live in a way that is 'inauthentic', we find ourselves restless till we settle down where we love. So, make some changes there!

- **Withdrawing from family and friends**- One does this because one is feeling overwhelmed, make a diary titled 'My positive Evenets and experiences 'dairy' and read it often, add in it often.

- **Being a mother IS transformative**, yes, but intensity can be relaxed with wisdom, it should be MORE of a gentle, accepting, celeberative! and embracing journey than one filled with too much uncomfortableness.

- **Loss of appetite or eating much more than usual**- When we eat too much, we need to ask ourselves, is it necessary?

- **Inability to sleep (insomnia**) or sleeping too much- It's best to make your environment beautiful, welcoming, and relaxed. Keep the temperature in your environment comfortable. Usually, villagers just have a hut to sleep in, no AC, nothing, so if you have an air conditioner, use it the bare minimum, be okay with different temperatures. Don't give in to artificial living too much.

- **Overwhelming fatigue or loss of energy**- This is normal, but if it gets too much, consult a doctor.

- **Reduced interest and pleasure in activities you used to enjoy**- This shouldn't happen but if it happens, make space for pleasure in your life always.

- **Intense irritability and anger**-Irritability and anger issues can be healed while talking and taking positive action.

- **Fear that you're not a good mother**- This fear is collective, if you are caring, sensitive, concerned for others needs and not self-obsessed, you are automatically a good woman and can be a good mother.

- **Feelings of worthlessness, shame, guilt, or inadequacy**-These are again collective fears. As an individual everyone is unique, beautiful, and good.

- **Diminished ability to think clearly, concentrate, or make decisions**— If this happens, try meditation.

- **Severe anxiety and panic attack**s- For panic attacks, consult your doctor. However, in order to avoid them, don't do anything you are afraid of doing, don't cross too many boundaries of others, be in nature and around beauty and familiarity. Too many strange lands lead to panic attacks.

- **Thoughts of harming yourself or your baby**-These thoughts are again collective, coming from some collective memory, or conditioning, always know what's YOUR thought and what isn't, this takes practice and being aware, and meditation.

'Before a woman a pregnant, she may be busy achieving as a student, or a focused career woman, however the real surrender and settling happens when she becomes a parent' even if for a while, eternity feels relaxed again' when the woman pauses and turns back to her true nature for a while.'

Summary of this chapter

'When someone elses happiness is your happiness that is love'

It is the effort of life bonding with life, it is sensitive, it is delicate it is the only feeling that lives and rests with us at the end of the day, the sweet moments of unconditional love, that is why, to chase anything real stops us from being in the moment And in this moment the gift is holy, eternal and pure.

10 ways I express and receive and notice uncondtional love are

1.

2.

3.

4.

5.

6.

7.

8.

9.

10

Gratitude moment

When we take responsibility for our lessons, our blessings have a way to make their presence felt in our Lives and moments. A home of the empress in the larger sense is not to be possessed but to be enjoyed. Think of a struggle for shelter. A home is meant to give us rejuvenation, refreshment, love, and warmth. It is a safe haven.

'In pregnancy the mother is the beat of the process. And the baby is the heart. Hence, revel by basking and relying and receiving all the support that nourishes you." Also whichever country or city you are living in, make sure to look at the good about the city and country.

For example Easily available stock for my requirements. Beautiful architecture access to parks where I can enjoy. All the wonderful Wonders of the world.

Whatever is good about your city do acknowledge it I gently open my heart to all the good my city, country has to offer from all the enriching support the world offers during pregnancy to the fruit and vegetable markets, to the beautiful fabrics I can wear, to the wonder ful clean temples, to the beautiful caring people, the cities activities obviously and naturally affect us so its important to be in the positive side willingly and play your role the best. Isn't it? A true fact.

As a pregnant woman you can acknowledge so much more, in fact the more you show gratitude the more happiness you feel. Every city has its own uniqueness about it. And one has to simply notice and shine a message of gratitude for its unique offering. I am understanding to the cities history and progress, and I try not to look for flaws but goodness.

Do you know when you complain less, you are more in the flow of your gratitude?

You can acknowledge even a healthy tree or freshness of one glass of water is enough to bring in gratitude? And then to bigger things. Imagine if we all started watering the plants of our city, we would realize the value of our existence, and presence and unique role in the wellbeing of our communities, we cant water the plants of the entire city but we can take care of our communities.

The value and gratitude of my relatives

In reality, Relatives are added family some close some far some near, some never met, but never the less they make our togetherness more resourceful and joyous and harmonious colorful And great full.

Whenever we truly receive a gift from a relative we give back our friendship. In short the trees are our relatives, the flowers are sisters the earth our true friend and relating is really a true gift, especially in honesty and truth. I love and respect my desire to relate to life joyfully and honestly.

Written on 2018 September

5 ways I appreciate my relatives are

1.

2.

3.

4.

5.

Message to the reader

Embracing the enriching empress in you. This chapter had a lot of information on health Mental physical and Emotional how very essential it is to find our center as a parent and especially as a pregnant parent? Obviously it begins with taking care of our physical health first beginning with cleansing our body of toxins cleansing our mind of clutter and our environment of it as well managing our hormones and inner and outer the more we are in harmony the closer we are to effortless bliss full experience that one so deserves during their pregnancy I give credits for this chapter to learning on all of this from different good sources and also my Child birth education you read a lot so far, and this chapter is the longest of the entire book because it has a lot of information for the reader on how to embrace the enriching empress in you however what if some days you cant? You may find it hard to well we all have those days, and not all days go in a certain way the more fresh, renewed and creative a day is, the more happier we will be, because in this big beautiful world honoring our creative selves is beautiful. You read on passages of making a journal to making art, how important it is to 'commune' with nature and communicate with your community. That actually creates the beautiful aura for your experience. No matter how much we will try to fit in other communities we always have our 'people to turn back to'. the poem sweet space came to me while I was writing this book, I sensed mothers give a beautiful reiki quite naturally, well at least most of them.

Activity for you

- Before You commit to this pregnancy, think of committing to a fabulous health routine, 2 years or 1 year before you decide to get pregnant, this will actually keep you mentally, emotionally, physically prepared when the time comes more beautifully.

Reflection: When women compare, or judge each other than celeberate each other's beauty and differences, we create more darkness in our society and culture'

Pregnancy Myth busted: Pregnant women don't need any special help during natural disasters and other emergencies"

What I intend to do:

Physically

- Swimming in summers(because I love it)
- Zumba(to enjoy the free flow of dancing)
- Yoga(to feel holistic in mind body)

Mental health

Host a few workshops for others in my community or those who are interested.

Avoid internet and media as much as I can.(I have done my share of surfing), and I realized I really don't need it anymore in my life, except for very occasional surfing thank god I am not addicted.

Stay Organised Don't collect/ and clutter. Buy/ only what I truly need.

Emotionally

- Don't hide suppress my emotions/ express them appropriately.
- Never beat myself for not doing 'enough'
- Look for creative ways to store food, that wont make you buy, every month.
- Buying your stock for 3 months is better than buying every month. If not 3, then 2.
- And, look at how much You need realistically, than following blindly social ways of being fulfilled
- To Begin with: You must make your list too!

Notes

1. What were some of the favourite lines from this chapter. How did it make you Feel?

_____

_____

_____

_____

_____

_____

_____

_____

_____

2. What insights did you receive to make your experience more enriching and meaningful?

_____

_____

_____

_____

_____

_____

_____

_____

_____

Gentle & Hopeful Chapter 6

Labor and Nutrition
To Beautiful Beginnings

Throughout this chapter you will find tools for a labor with ease its so important to know and understand the comfort measures and have knowledge about how to make this process a process of ease and helpful for the mother from support system to understanding the stages of labor well if you are a parent and you have gone through the stage yourself you could make your skills better by remembering them and supporting your own child in their pregnancy whatever calls you is fine below are some common ailments that one can experience during their pregnancy from morning sickness to heartburn to headache some common diseases to make sure to keep bay are hypertension obesity, heart attack and many other ailments,it arises from not taking the right measures during your Pregnancy so lets delve and explore the helpful measures for a successful birth.

Congratulations and Celeberations

Thank you, Lord Shiva for the protection, Lakshmi for the abundance and grace abundance I have and grace I can imbibe from you. Keeping divine in mind puts me in a position to remember that I am telling myself and my baby I respect your birth And I honor having you Around.

Gratitude sutras poem

1st month

Rama for the Clarity.

2nd month

Radha for the remembrance of sweetness of being loved.

3rd month

Krishna for the lotus feet and perception.

4th month

Shakti for the acceptance and dance of love.

5th month

Mira for the sensitivity and devotion in love.

6th month

Lakshman for the brotherhood.

7th month

Sita for the patience

8th month

Ganpati for removing obstacles andbringing prosperity

9ᵗʰ month

Goddess Saraswati for learning.

Strength for the Recovery months

10ᵗʰ month

Durga for action and compassion.

11ᵗʰ month

Lord Buddha for creativity, restoration and truth.

12ᵗʰ month

Mother Mary for Unconditional Love.

13ᵗʰ month.

Mother and Father earth, for helping, protecting, nurturing and guiding through this beautiful process.

14ᵗʰ month :

My loving husband and friends for uplifting and keeping me happy and hopeful.

May these qualities remind me to go with compassion in my work, life, and learning experiences through schooling, living, and remembering.

Pondering on Divine Timing

There is divine timing for everything, a child could have been born too early before his or her time, but a mother knows when its time, a parent knows instinctively and even better thoughtfully when it is time, hence the preparation for divine timing can be either full of celebration or it can be full of anxiety.

When we trust *divine Timing* it is sacred and we aren't exploiting time We remember how to act in it And we play well And we prepare gracefully and lovingly. Don't miss the divine timing.

When you know its time to act, AFFIRMING- Divine timing works in my life effortlessly and celebratefully my preparation is graceful and amazing and I smile a lot and I am in gratitude for the divine timings role in my life. I love honor and invite divine timing in my life.

Don't feel guilty for not acting that way in the past, acknowledge and remember that difficult lessons can turn into blessings with time patience and trust.

I am in gratitude for many times this has worked in my life, for example my intuition to start working on this book, however I wish I worked on it much earlier, but I am working on it now and adding in the last bit tiny details of it which means that I am improving and maybe in tune with my timing.

If I feel good about something, I am in tune
If I feel negative I am not.
If I feel nervous I am not
If I feel light I am good.

The role of the umbilical cord

The umbilical cord is a tube like structure that connects. The fetus to the mothers placenta, the vein carries oxygenated blood and nutrients from the placenta to the fetus through the abdomen, and the arteries remove waste products.

It contains three vessels and two arteries and one vein which carries blood back to the baby. The blood in the arteries contain waste products such as CO2 from the baby's metabolism O2 is transported from red blood cells in your circulation, across the placenta to the baby in the umbilical vein. In addition to oxygen, the umbilical cord transports nutrients from the placenta to the baby.

The vessels in the umbilical cord have a protective coating called Whartons Jelly. And the cord is coiled like a spring so the baby is free to move around. The coiling of the cord has usually established itself by week nine and is usually in a counterclockwise direction.

The cord is attached to the center of the placenta, although sometimes its attached near the edge. Very occasionally it divides, into its separate vessels before finally entering the placenta. The cord is usually under 1 inch in diameter and 23 60 cm long. Which is twice the length needed to ensure that there are no problems in delivery.

After delivery. The cord vessels close by themselves. The arteries close first, helped by their thicker muscular walls this prevents blood loss to the placenta from your baby. The umbilical vein, closes slightly later by 3-4 minutes. This allows blood to continue to return to your baby during the first few minutes of life. As a result, many feel that there is a slight delay, before clamping the cord can be beneficial to the baby. There are no nerves within the cord, so cutting the cord, after delivery is painless procedure for your baby.

Also if you have a belief that you don't deserve to be healthy happy and fulfilled let it go now, because your cord will connect with the baby. Also feel safe to follow your desires, and respect others as well.

Umbilical cord connects the baby and the mother in a loving bond' hence her habits, perceptions of the process and world does mildly affect the baby or more'

In chakra psychology the navel chakra is connected to the power chakra, when you feel alive happy safe to follow your own happiness, imagine a confused mother, her body cant select or focus where to go what to go, don't be led by others that is weakness be led by your own self that is strength and true power. I had tears in my eyes when I got this last guidance in my mind, about the sacred umbilical cord connection it is truly sacred.

Worth waiting for "what I'm waiting for is not what someone else is waiting for yet, in this wait there is gentleness,celebration and lack of pretense, awareness in trust that is needed coupled with deeds and seeds sown, for the wait to turn to fruition" "We can spend hours spent in collecting seeds of worry, or holding on to wisdom and courage."

What is divine timing?

It is the time you know you are doing the right thing and are experiencing goodness because you sowed the seed of what you are harvesting now.

Divine timing means you trust, have faith and don't let fears block you progress passion and persistence it is flavor of heroic faith, and the dance of wellbeing and less worrying about the future but having confidence in it.without using the language of worry.

Why are some births not successful ?

It is so essential to remember that if you have the amenities, you must make proper use of them, which is common sense, people who don't have access to good quality hospitals or centers should worry, but people who have access to all good should not worry at all. 'I let go of excuses if god has blessed me with good'.

1. **Lack of GOOD knowledge** about birth is SO important. As an intelligent and sensitive person, it is imperative to get knowledge about birth, even if reading about it doesn't interest you, It is much better than obsessively readyng about other things. In fact, I believe that reading about BIRTH should come in every intelligent child's curriculum. It should be included in the education of both girls and boys from the age of 18. Sexual education and BIRTH education is not only important, it is essential for intelligent and sensitive people. This avoids so much trauma, drama and problems which come out of lack of knowledge, or understanding of uneasiness during pregnancy. Knowledge is not only power, it contributes to being aware.

2. **POVERTY--** Not enough money to sustain through the pregnancy. So many families experience this

because money should be an important subject for all parents, do you earn it? But can't keep it? Earn it but spend it? whatever the problem is, you must find out.

3. **Postpartum depression** is about saving energy, emotional health, physical and psychological health. Engage in all activities which Contribute to this. Otherwise, depression happens, especially if you are prone to it. Don't get invited by depression, Get invited by the willingness to Recover.

4. **Become your own best friend**- talk to yourself or talk openly to people you Love. Remembering to become a BLESSING from being a BURDEN will take time but nothing's really a burden for a good friend.

5. **Give yourself a TIMELINE** to recover. Don't get into the recovery mood. Always recovering, always healing, always vulnerable--this attitude Invites more depression and less willingness and strength to MOVE through life.

6. **Practice kindness**, gentleness and grace will FOLLOW.

7. **LOOK AT THE bright side**. If you are recovering, learn to celebrate.

8. **NOTICE YOUR UNIQUE PATTERN**- Notice, and see, if you withdraw abnormally or you become shy, overcome these patterns by telling yourself, YOU are alive, it's natural to be a little apprehensive with a new way of living, but you can do it, because

you matter, people love you, and no one wants to see me ill or vulnerable.

9. **CONNECT** with other women, and see how they deal with the weight of postpartum depression.

Be aware of risk of falls and slipping

Most mothers are fiercely protective of their children. However they aren't careful with themselves during pregnancy you have to manage this one correctly risk of falling.

Falling down the stairs is the most common accident, if you live in a home with stairs manage how you will do your up down before your pregnancy, or be aware of slippery stairs.

During this time, if you spend your time indoors your home needs to be spic and span away from lethal doses of chemicals, be aware of your own body and how it feels inside outside, during the night and day, when the baby is developing you need to be alert aware and attentive. Best is to be in a room which does not require you to climb so many stairs, this helps in your pregnancy enormously, if you do a balance of indoor outdoor, otherwise those who have a terrace garden don't need to go down, often, however being aware of slipping is very important.

We can have during our pregnancy because, we start believing we are super important or we need to be cared for, any extra energy we ask for will have a consequence, we receive a lot during pregnancy if we are lucky, but if you can maintain your self respect which is very important, then often you wont have a character slip, which will annoy you or others. When you know you are slipping, you are doing extra than you can give or you are going against your own character or integrity, immediately get back to your grounding and what you are really wanting asking for. Irritating and annoying others can furiate yourself and others, in times of over whelment just communicate clearly. Ill try to maintain my respect for myself and my baby and practice great fullness its natural to not be perfect but its not natural to be of annoyance and extra demanding.

- You can slip
- You can fall

Solution alert aware attentive of the environment you reside in, and just pay attention to how your body feels.

The extra weight you gain,
Worries
Fear
Scattering
Complaining
No gratitude
Unhealthy eating
Too much passivity or thinking.
And no appreciation.
And no desire to progress.
No mindfulness.
Or heartfullness
Creates,
Mindlessness

Benefits of juices during pregnancy

1. Benefits of Beetroot Juice

- Helps with iron deficiency and anemia. The fetus requires iron to develop which is which is why pregnant women are advised to take iron supplements. Beetroot juice is one of the best pregnancy juices to help boost iron.

- Helps with constipation. Constipation is common during pregnancy. Beetroot juice is a natural cure for this.

- Lowers blood pressure. High blood pressure increases the risk of premature delivery and can cause several other complications.

- Beetroot, carrot, and apple juice (1 carrot, ½ beetroot, 1 apple)

2. Carrot Juice

Carrots are rich in beta-carotene, iron, magnesium, B vitamins, potassium, magnesium, and more. Pregnant women shouldn't consume more than a glass of carrot juice daily.

Benefits of carrot Juice

- Improves skin. Skin changes are one of the side effects of pregnancy. Carrot juice is amazing for the skin. It reduces scarring, hydrates skin, and evens skin tone.

- Good for teeth, hair, nails.

- Digestive problems during pregnancy are commonplace. They can get worse during the last stage of pregnancy due to pressure applied to the uterus by the growing baby.

- Reduces blood pressure.

- Blood pressure juice (¼ beetroot, 2 carrots)

3. Cucumber Juice

- Cucumbers are great sources of vitamin A, vitamin C, potassium, manganese, folate, and more. The best cucumbers are firm to the touch and have a dark color.

- Benefits of cucumber juice

- Regulates blood pressure. Minerals and sodium in cucumber help to regulate blood pressure.

- Helps tighten skin. The skin tightening properties of cucumber are exactly what pregnant women need.

- It is a diuretic and prevents swelling. Swelling can become a problem during the third trimester. Cucumber juice helps to neutralize this problem.

- Teeth and gum problems. Cucumber juice neutralizes the acids in the mouth preventing gum and teeth problems that are very common during pregnancy.

- Cucumber and apple juice (1 large cucumber, ½ apple)

4. Pumpkin Juice

- Pumpkin juice is rich in beta-carotene, vitamin C, vitamin A, potassium, magnesium, and more.

- Benefits of Apple Juice

- Helps with sleeping disorders.

- Strengthens the immune system.

- Lowers cholesterol levels.

- Improves skin.

- Orange and apple juice (3 oranges, 1 apple)

- Adding water to fresh juice dilutes it to make it easier for the body to handle. Drink fruit juices on an empty stomach. It easiest if you drink fruit juices first thing in the morning. Vegetable juices can be consumed at any time. Although, it is recommended that you drink them 20 minutes before a meal.

- Try drinking one or more of these pregnancy juices daily.

- Do not go on a juice fast while pregnant.

Morning sickness	Eat high protein foods, and several meals daily, avoid fried foods, sip soda water, get out of bed daily, drink spearmint, raspberry leaf, or peppermint tea.
Heartburn	Avoid foods known to cause heartburn, fried and highly seasoned foods, drink water between meals, instead of during meals. Sit upright when eating.
Headache	Get plenty of rest and sleep, eat regularly, drink plenty of fluids, take a bath or get a massage.
Difficulty sleeping	Drink warm milk at bedtime, avoid coffee, do relaxation exercises, decrease lights.

Fatigue	Eat well, and regularly, get enough rest and sleep. Exercise daily.
Constipation	Drink 64-lt or more of fluids daily. Eat raw fruits and vegetables.

Abdominal	Allergies	Anemia?	Appetite/excess	Arthiritis	Asthma	Bad breath
Multiple sclerosis	Nausea	Nervous issues	Osteoporosis	Paralysis	Parkinsons	Sciatica
Blood pressure	Body odor	Breast	dizziness	Cancer	Eczema	Skin diseases
Skin issues	Bites	Sprains	Tuberculosis	Uterus problems	vomittin	Warts
Obesity	Food poisoning	Gas	Respiratory problems	Gland problems	Gum problems	headaches
Arthritic fingers	Diabities	Hypertension	Morning sickness	Constipation	Amnesia	
Hip pain	Hyperactivity	Indigestion	Injuries	Insomnia	Miscarriage	mouth

Labor is a time when you realize that you went through the entire 9 month journey well its even time to count how many times you fell sick where and why, and next time take care for the next pregnancy, or just become more aware and attentive, we don't let a snake bite us twice do we?

A major or minor illness brings us to realisation about what we had ignored, supressed, left alone, since long, and when we face it, and take charge and allow the blessing to blossom from it'. See any illness as a cry from your body to listen to it more compassionately, emotionally intimately and kindly'. An illness didn't occur to make you depressed, but to make you more aware of 'When you change the way you view birth, what you view and how you experience it changes'. You cant heal in the same enviroment that made you sick'.

Every injury that happens to us makes us more aware of our body mind. It's a gentle opportunity to be closer to more self care and wisdom. So lets see how to use this table. Now look above and see from the list above if you had any of the problems above *what was the intensity? why was I exposed here? what lifestyle habit caused it? how am I living?* its important to be more careful and alert of your surroundings. Do you remember what all you did to recover and how do you celebrate your recovery no Many people learn to let go, and get back to normal tasks immediately, but we need here is more gracefully.

Gratitude for Recovery

I allow myself wholesome loving caring recovery. "When I am in gratitude for my recovery am in gratitude for my self care as well" never allow yourself to be treated like a space –goat someone who is doing life a favor to have a baby, if you want to do it do it with awareness love celebration and gladness. they say you get a little spaced out during pregnancy, because it's a normal.

Why a person spaces out distraction, lack of sleep, stress, fatigue, seizure. we become space-goats when we ignore, deny, judge, blame. Blindly do something. Don't let our space be guarded or let ourselves be walked upon remember to speak up for your boundaries when someone over steps.

We become responsible when we See, Accept, Embrace, Trust, Love, Aliveness. Let our space be guarded. I learn to gracefully recover give thanks and celebrate my recovery. Make a list of all the times you had a minor or major recovery and send smiles, to the sun in your heart, for the healing power of the body, good nutrition and positive I respect and cherish my body's healing power how it heals from ailments and diseases is the sign of its magnificence and wonder and beauty. Beyond what the eyes can see The inner healing departments work beautifully so I can feel healthy again *I acknowledge this gentle healing dependable power of my body.*

Self aware chart

What happened?	How and where?	When?	How long it took you to recover and what all you did to recover?	Positive improvements Negative spiral behavior.
Sprained my leg	During a mountaineering trail trek.	6 months ago		Positive improvement was I learnt to move a with more awareness and learnt to be more gentle with myself, I was more alert and attentive.
			From April- july I used leg sprain, pain killer medicines.	Negative spiral would be, I would go back to Hyper activity and uncaring movement

Breathing correctly

Food Mother & Baby

Do you know sometimes a child falls asleep during and breastfeeding? Its not a sign of worry because the child is either sleepy or got enough of the milk he wants and the milk actually promotes healthy sleep as the milk has got special healing properties that promote deep sleep and formation of the cells of the baby's body.

When the baby is getting enough milk, The baby starts feeding with open eyes and focused alert expression. Your breasts feel softer and less full at end of feeding. If the baby has fallen asleep and his hands are open and relaxed and her arms hand down limply if her hands or face look tense, she may be still hungry.

Welcoming graceful eating during my pregnancy

The role of eating in my pregnancy well We get used to eating food in a certain way For example, in my example, food was always served to me as I lived in hostels, and colleges.so I never had the privilege of cooking my own meals. It's a cultural message that is given to us, when we are young to be irresponsible with our food choices. Where we are fed and you can get fed up of this. The culture of restaurants and heavy eating never appealed to me. I did really enjoyed my cooking classes.

Pregnancy is a time when we can learn to discern and form new ways of treating our food, our environment, and for others It defines us a whole lot and it is personal for everyone. Use this time to really pray to the sacred for what you have, and not be scared to change your eating habits!

Well the brain learns to eat in two ways, **Aggressively (primal)** – This is what we see in wild animals, hunters etc. We had this instinct because of hunger pangs and dying of hunger. So, if you have food and healthy food consider practising moderation and awareness in consumption, and try to nurture, and be guided to select the best food, eat with your mind body and soul Eat with love, on your plate, be conscious of your quantity. There is no need to invest time in eating aggressively it could affect the baby. Food should make me feel alive fresh, and cared for. I feel happy being a part of this amazing rich world with so much variety to choose from.

The entire body actually makes use of the energy our mouth chews and sends to the stomach to digest, so actually, its wiser to ask yourself how does the body feel, after eating? (not just the stomach) Intutitve thought.

Variety with different tastes is natural for the young infant turned into toddler to be introduced to, however organic nutrition is naturally priority for their developing bodies.

- Sweet fruits
- Sour lemon
- Will resist bitter(natural), bitter gourd and others.
- And neutral, nuts, seeds and milk.
- Spicy(will take time to adjust to spicy)

Teaching your baby good manners will be the foundation of good health from the very beginning this means you can teach your baby the differenciation between tastes, and as his intelligence is developing his/her response-ability does improve. I respect my Childs developing abilities.

Tip: Also in the enviroment you eat, really makes a difference in the way you digest so surround yourself with a loving kind and nourishing enviroment.

Food basic for your infant/ toddler.

Start with small servings. If your child is still hungry, help your child to explore issues like how to know when they're full.

Have you had Enough?

Do you feel full?

You can help children learn that some foods may start to taste better when they've been tried several times.

Help children learn to focus on the taste of what they eat, so they are conscious of the sensations and pleasure it gives them. Teach them about vegetables and fruits you could create songs around it. You should notice what the child likes.

Never force anything down their mouth. They resist it by throwing it out,denoting they are full. Help children learn to be polite, and say no by teaching them basic signs.Feeding them in nice places and spaces, and in one place everyday, notice where the child is happier eating, knowing which enviroment your child likes, will help you to help him feed.

Monday	Tuesday	Wednesday	Thursday	Friday
Rice porrige	Khichdi	Idli with dal	Apple stew	Avacado
Carot puree	Boiled egg	Pumpkin seed powder with fruits	Curd rice	Peach puree and strawberry
Rice with dal	Apple puree	roti	Boiled vegetable	Banana puree with nuts
channa	banana	Lentil soup		Ccconut puree with fruits

Basic Food schedule for one Year Old toddler

Infant only requires sleep and eat but they even require a good sensory stimulation and contact. Good sensory diet for growing up infant toddler. Requires more of natural light than artificial light. Fresh oxygen for their skin Good food for the development of their body's basic energy. And gentle nourishing food and sleep environment Is what basically an infant requires to grow a healthy brain body and bones. Good emotional diet as they grow up is healthy social contact. Friends and healthy play mates and school friends.

Prevent heart dis-ease by

Quitting smoking get active maintain a healthy weight control you cholesterol drink alcohol in modernization and don't worry about the 'heart' just let it beat on its own do you worry? just take care of the above.

When walking 'walk' when eating 'eat'- Zen proverb

Overcoming one fear each day is fine, Sharing love with one person in a quality way each day is fine, Giving one or few quality smiles per day is fine, Opening your heart gently toward one person per day is fine. Giving and receiving one compliment per day is fine, Have we noticed, how much we care to exchange with life being happy and in gratitude for the roles we play in our lives in a quality way is better than paying attention to roles we play with no heart. Our attention goes where our heart is, well so it is with 'food'.

In a healthy way?

In a joyful way?

Well same goes with food, we eat according to what we are, and feel. There is no competition in food, friendship and family. These are loving gifts from our creator.

When we naturally love, care, we notice that we learn to tune in our capacity with what we can truly handle, rather than artificially inflating anything our appetite or ego.

'The way we treat food speaks a lot about us in a way the relationship I have with my food, will affect the relationship my children will have with their food.

Baby foods

4-6 months

Banana and avacadoes. Coconut oil or seaseme oil spoon feed. All purees, vegetable and fruit mixed Homemade ice creams if you can make.

6-8 months

Raw mashed food cooked pureed fruits such as peaches, pears apples and berries with cream. Chic peas is very good protein. Mashed scrambled eggs. Carrots, beets with butter.

8-12 months

Creamed vegetable soups. Dairy such as yoghurt, cheese cream custards. Same as the above.

Around 1 year.

Grains and legumes, properly soaked and cooked. Babies can eat milk porridge and oatmeal. Crispy nut butters. Leafy green vegetables. Well cooked with butter. Citrus fruit, fresh and organic whole egg, cooked.

Barley porridge

Warm your heart with this humble porridge made from the versatile cereal grain, barley. Have it as a light breakfast or when you want to satisfy your 11 o'clock hunger pangs. Soak this grain overnight to reduce it's cooking time.

Ingredients

- 2 tbsp barley, soaked overnight

- 4 cups water

- 1 tsp of jaggery

- A pinch of crushed cardamom (elaichi)

- Fistful of nuts such as almonds and walnuts, crushed

Method

1   Wash the soaked barley and pressure cook it with 3 cups of water for 2-3 whistles.

2   After it cools, grind the barley pearls with a little bit of water

3   Now, heat this paste with some water and a little milk, if required. Keep stirring so that no lumps are formed. Add the jaggery a pinch of salt and the crushed nuts. Consume hot with your favorite fruits.

Plate of Oats Idli

Ingredients

- 2 cups oats
- 1 cup yoghurt
- 1 cup wheat rava
- 2 cups water
- 2 tbsp coriander leaves for tempering
- 1 tbsp ghee
- 1 tbsp black gram
- Mustard
- 8-10 curry leaves

Method

1. Take a nonstick pan and heat it.

2. Once it is hot, roast the oats for about 2-3 minutes on a low flame and keep it aside. Once it cools down make it into a powder in a blender.

3. Now add ghee to a pan. When the ghee is hot, add tempering ingredients, and stir it well

4. Now add the vegetables and coriander leaves and cook for about 2 minutes.

5. Add the rava and sauté on a low flame for another couple of minutes.

6. Place this mixture in a bowl and add blended oats, salt to taste, water, and curd.

7. Mix it well to turn it into Idli batter.

8. Once the idli molds are greased, add drops of ghee, pour the batter, and cook for 20 minutes. Serve hot with coconut or peanut chutney.

Ajwain halwa

This traiditonal recipie makes use of dry ginger and ajwain, both known to facilitate digestion and aid lactation. Use jaggery instead of sugar to sweeten this *halwa* to make it more healthy and earthy.

Ingredients

- 1 cup whole wheat flour

- ½ cup pure pure ghee

- 1/2 cup jaggery

- ½ tsp powdered ajwain

- ¼ tsp dry ginger powder

- A pinch of cardamom powder

- Dry fruits of your choice for garnishing

- Filtered water

Method

1. Heat ghee in a thick bottomed pan. Add whole wheat flour and roast on medium flame until it turns golden brown and the ghee starts to separate. Be sure to separate all the lumps

2. Now add in powdered carom (ajwain) seeds and dry ginger (saunth). Stir the mixture for a few minutes. Add jaggery and mix well.

3. Pour the water and stir the mixture. Cook till it thickens in consistency Remove from the stove. Garnish the halwa with dry fruits and a pinch of cardamom powder. Serve hot.

4. Ajwain helps in digestion, and helps increase breastmilk production in mothers.

Glass of pumpkin milk

Ingredints

- Pumpkin seeds crushed

- You could add almonds if you wish

- Warm milk

- Raisins

- Soak the almonds overnight

Method

1. Make pumpkin seed powder.

2. Mix in the mixie with milk with warm milk, add some saffron and haldi to it.

3. Enjoy the health benefits of almond pumpkin milk.

4. The combination of almond and pumpkin is amazing. it gives you health benefits of both almond and pumpkin together, and viola there you go, an amazing milk combination and both are excellent for pregnancy and breastfeeding.

Methi garlic soup

Fenugreek leaves have long been used as a milk boosting food.

Ingredients

- 1 cup fresh fenugreek leaves or methi.

- ½ cup onion, finely chopped.

- 1 ripe tamato, finely chopped.

- 3-4 garlic clove minced.

- 2 cups water.

- Salt and pepper powder to taste.

- 2 cup seaseme seed oil.

Method

1. Heat oil in a pan, add chopped onion, garlic and sauté until onions turn translucent.

2. Now add the tomatoes and cook for a few minutes.

3. Now add cleaned and chopped Methi leaves and sauté until greens wilt.

4. Add two cups of diluted water, salt and simmer for a while.

5. Blend half the quantity of and add the rest to the soup, and simmer

6. For another 15 minutes add pepper powder to taste. Methi is excellent for breastfeeding and it enhances the breast milk immediately after consumption

Spinach Broccoli pistachio soup

Ingredients

- 1 cup salted pistachios,

- 3 spring onions

- 1 tsp olive oil

- 1 garlic clove

- Coconut cream/milk

- Sea salt and pepper

- 1 head broccoli

Method

1. Fry the onion spring onions and chopped garlic in olive oil, over a low heat until tender and sweet but not browned.

2. Boil coconut milk or cream in a separate pan.

3. Soak the pistachios overnight and make a puree of it in a processor.

4. Steam the broccoli if you don't have a steamer fill a pot with some water and add.

5. Broccoli in boiling water. Once it boils, add it to your coconut milk, or water, as per your choice!

6. Set aside a couple of small florets for decorating if you wish.

7. Blend until smooth in a blender or food processor.

8. Season to taste with salt. Spinach has high levels of calcium, iron, Vitamin K and A and folate. Which are excellent for breastfeeding mothers.

Some delicious homemade jam options

Much information about farming taken from local farmers, and some from, bottled fruit bottled peaches for you and your newborn.

Ingredients

- 4-5 firm peaches

- Honey

- Water

Equipment

- Large sauce pan

- Sharp knife

- Preserving jar with lids

Remove skin from peaches if they are difficult to peel, put the fruit in boiling water for about 30 seconds the skins should then slip off easily. Cut the peaches into half and carefully remove the stones.

Place honey, sugar, or jaggery in water to boil, until it is dissolved. You can add a little mint too.

Fill the jars with fruit.After it is boiled, ladle in hot sugar syrup or honey, or caramelized sugar with nuts, until the jar is full. Seal the jars with lids and store in a dark cool place. You can make jars with figs, cherries, pears, and plums.

Fresh plum and apple chutney

Ingredients

- Cooking apples

- Plums

- Onions

- Ginger

- Raisins

- Light brown sugar

- Salt

- Allspice

- Ground cloves

- Ground cinnamon

- Apple cider vinegar

Start by peeling, coring, and cutting the apples.Wash the plums and chop them roughly, taking care to remove all the stones.

Take the skin off the onions before slicing them and grating the ginger.

Pull all the fresh ingredients into a preserving pan or large saucepan and add the raisins, salt, sugar, and apple cider vinegar.

What is labor?

Labor is defined as the period time your cervix begins to open thin, until the moment your placenta emerges. It's a time warp of chaos, resting movement and preparation.

- When you arrive at the hospital

- Your family member will be given forms to Fill.

- You will be asked to wear a hospital gown (or you can carry your own).

- Your pubic hair needs to be shaved, so get it waxed or shave it before you go if you are uncomfortable with the hospital shaving.

- Usually hospitals provide enema, where a tube is inserted in the anus, and fluid fleshes the bowels.

- This avoids the passing of stool during birth.

- Often after enema the contractions become stronger, as it aids the process of birth more quicker.

- There after you will be taken to the delivery room During labor, your blood pressure will be taken as well, the nurse will also take your temperature

- Sometimes the woman is given medication to progress in her labor, if youd like to progress without too much medication, try to practice correct posture, proper breathing.

- And have your inner strength support you.

Labor support

It is recommended that a woman has a bath before pregnancy.

Understanding labor support

Understanding the labor support gives us insight into the support a mother will need through each phase and stage.

Labor has three stages

Early labor- This is the longest part of most labors and mothers are often tempted to rush into the hospital or birth center. If there is an emergency, the woman should rush to the hospital. It is critical for a mother to spend time at home doing normal activities and resting. These normal activities include resting, eating, sleeping, drinking, and going about daily life. Resting is very crucial at this time. Get your therapeutic ice packs, practice tightening and releasing uterine muscles lightly and spend time near a trees and flowers can strengthen and soothe you.

What is happening in early labor?

Pressure in lower abdomen, period cramps pressure or tightening in the lower back. in very difficult labor which needs extra support and energy you need to give more time, rest as much as possible nurture by eating drinking and warm baths. Drug induced rest.

Active labor- During this time, the woman needs more support, she may benefit from massages position changes and visualisations and other comfort measures. The laboring woman should find and be aware of labor positions, and practice her breathing techniques and drink enough lukewarm water. Castor oil is recommended too.

What is most important for this stage?

Deep breathing, and good posture and preparation for nearing the final stage. In difficult active phase give her more time increase activity changing positions, walking, nipple stimulaton, acupressure comfort measures bath shower or massage or breathing etc.

Transition- This part of labor is typically the shortest and the most intense, extra stimulation makes it harder for the mother to cope with her contractions. Support people should minimize movement, touch, talking, lights and noise. Conversations and talks should be kept minimum, the Laboring women should have motivating statements around her like, laboring women should motivate the to be mother, and the baby's head should be pointing towards the cervix at this stage!

During this time you may be wanting to hit the toilet there will be bloody vaginal discharge, hot cold, shaky legs, an urge to vomit, and a deep yearning to take a nap. Hence it is so essential to try to do all this in the previous stages, so you can be present at this final stage.

You still need to maintain your good breathing, and good posture try holding orange peels on your hands and squeeze them tight like your making orange juice, your palms need something to do before the baby is out, and will distract your attention from what's happening beneath there.

Motivate her with words and affirmations such as

You can do it!
Push darling!
You're almost there!
You're a brave mom!
Take her name 'Name', focus on breathing, you can do it!
We are going to see your baby soon!

Positions for labor

How easily can I breathe in this position?
Do my legs feel strong in this position?
Do I feel strained in this position?
Does my pelvic region feel open and relaxed in this position?
Does this position connect me with pull of gravity?
Be in the position that feels perfect for you.

Pain experience in labor may be due to.

Increased stress anxiety or fear

Stretching and distension of vagina, vulva, perineum and labia- tissues are stretching as the fetus is making a descent. Women often experience a burning sensation while the stretching is occurring.

Decreased oxygen supply to the uterus- the physiology of a contraction itself temporarily diminishes the oxygen available to the uterine muscle. We experience pain when any of our muscles are suffering from lack of oxygen. This very process is why slow steady breathing is encouraged all through labor and why breath holding for more than 5 seconds should be discouraged.

Effacement and dilation of cervix- with effective labor contractions, the size and shape of a woman's cervix changes to allow passage to the fetus.

Take care of these above problems, by exposing yourself to enough outdoor in the last month, sitting outdoor, using cold and hot packs, and resting.

P.s and here we are talking about a successful 9 month journey, from conception to completion, and also, much more'.

Tip and advises to have normal delivery

Eat frequent and small meals throughout the day.

Include a wholesome balanced meal for breakfast, lunch, and dinner.

- Do one thing at a time, don't multitask.
- Keep your mind and body in sync.
- Exercise, learn gentle meditation.
- Practice kindness.
- Don't force your body to do anything.
- Eat enough fruits

- Keep your thighs and vaginal muscles, strong with Kegels and massage.
- Include milk and milk products in your diet.
- Avoid being too much homebound, connection with outdoor and nature will be beneficial.
- Avoid foods that increase acidity.
- Eat dates and prunes.
- And red raspberry leaf tea.
- Keep away from danger or worry.
- See video of normal delivery.
- Practice ice therapy and warm towel therapy often during the labor month to prepare your body.
- Remember happy sensations. Like feel of cold water,
- or the taste of something nice.
- Think of your babies comfort a lot when the baby is in the womb,
- Think of how you could make a comfortable environment for the baby.
- Keep your space welcoming, musical, and positive. And filled with your love.
- Receive love from your parents.
- Think of what gives you joy!
- Practice simplicity.
- Bond with nature.
- Keep your skin happy.

Skin to skin

Skin is space/surrender, kindness in nurturing your skin is your space and your unique color, design and beauty, so will your babies, in motherhood the skin relaxes and surrender to the baby's skin naturally, our skin cannot tottally relax otherwise, in situations where we feel threatened.

Gentle affirmation

I love and respect the mantle that protects my body, I let go of any fear or threat, coming from outside toward me or my baby, All is well inside and outside. Mostly all threats are imagined and come out of fear, or imagining situations which don't exist yet.

Immediately after birth, baby's sense organs, reflexes, hormonal response all are designed to help the baby initiate the breast crawl do you know the baby in the uterus with every contraction, the baby feels this pressure against its body. The pressure against the baby's feet initiates the step reflex which in turn helps the baby. Step or dance his or her way through the womb. At the moment of the birth the skin 2 skin is very essential, as it elicits a complex bath of hormones and is essential for the baby to feel skin to skin provides temperature regulation, hormonal, metabolic, and neurological these 3 are essential to the ' health of the infant' stimulation and calming to prepare the baby to breastfeed.

Babies are placed near the mothers cheek and breasts, so that the baby can kiss the baby and also facilitate the custom of saying a loving message to the baby's ears.

The baby is kept very alert and responsive soon after delivery and hence is at his or her best instinctive level. Touch is a strong stimulus for Neurodevelopment.

The first skin to skin usually lasts until the baby finishes its first breastfeed. 'The meeting of preparation with opportunity generates the offspring we call luck'

Remember, sometimes, a thousand moments
of pain or discomfort
lead to having a baby, but now even the pain
can actually reveal a thousand moments of joy
we can experience.
Pain and pleasure are part of life. Yet, they are
transient,
don't label everything. Just love it and
let it pass.
You be a rainbow in the sky!

Gentle and positive Affirmations for
healthy delivery.
I allow only positive thoughts to be around my
baby, my body and me.
Life delivers me the confidence to carry
through with support and strength
I carry calmness in me, joy in my flesh, grace
in my veins, and passion in my heart, for
I hope it all goes well.
I am a container of confidence, life, and grace.
I carry love, joy, and patience, as my baby is
growing and resting inside me.
I find forgiveness cocoon me and carry
me through

Instead of wonder how much Birth will hurt,
Birth in a state of 'wonder'
There is no way to be a perfect mother but a
million ways to be a good one
How is your pregnancy Enviroment? Could you
contribute to local your hospital in some way?
Did you take your birthing classes by now?
My birthing room in the hospital is filled with
freshness, flowers and faith

Note to parents: Please consider taking a respiratory
health check-up before pregnancy as this is more likely to
help you have a normal delivery.

Do you like the hygiene of your Hospital?

Normal delivery: Comes out when ready with an
encouraging gentle push. Balanced immune system.

Respiratory problems- No smoking Quit travelling, or lessen it, a year or six months before pregnancy begins. Balance lifestyle, organic living, less eating out, balanced eating, less exposure to harsh chemicals.

Being in the now and breathing

REVERANCE: Having deep respect for something, in this case, your breath.

EMBRACING- Hold someone closely in arms, meaning to affection.

TRUTHFUL- being honest with yourself and others.

HARMONY- The combination of simultaneously sounded musical notes to produce a pleasing effect. How nice, a good breath should feel harmonious and musical.

So when you're losing your breath, your losing your music
'When you own your breath, no one steals your peace'

Caring Breath of life

Breath is being reverent, embracing, aligned to harmony. The mother and child are connected via breath to the mother like breath, voice, and heartbeat.

In this kind of closeness, embrace, and allow stillness to enrich you via breath in the moment, heartbeat to make you aware of how delicate life is and closeness to make you aware of how precious your health is for the child and you is going to be for the child, honor every life, little, big, or small, because one thing we can't fool is the wisdom of good healing fresh breath. And when we respect the breath we respect oxygen, food and pleasure and we come in contact with our true self within. **Intention-** To respect and honor my breath where you come from. and your breath.

Deep cleansing breath- Slow Breathing

Take an organizing breath—a big sigh as soon as the contraction begins.... focus your attention.

Slowly inhale through your nose and exhale through your mouth, allowing all your air to flow out with a sigh....

- With each exhale, focus on relaxing a different part of your body (see Relaxation Techniques).

- Waist level breathing. To help you relax and get a good night's sleep:

- Relax your mind and body in a warm bath or shower before bed.

- Learn relaxation exercises and breathing techniques.

- Limit your daytime sleeping.

- And also try to breathe only till the level of the waist.

Birth plan

A birth plan is what you want to ideally happen and then take the measures to make it happen. Sometimes it works, many times it does not but it depends on the quality of support you gather and enrich, and the correct tips you follow to have your birth. In case there is an emergency its understood plans can change.

During puushing and birth we would like to avoid.	During labor we would like to avoid	During pushing and birth we would like to avoid	After birth for baby we would like.	After birth for baby we would like.
Dim lights and conversations quiet. Please don't offer medications. Help with position guidance.	Medications Or C section.	Epistomy	Warm compress to help tissues stretch. Normal delivery.	We would like to give our baby bath at home Or Husband and family will be with me entire time.
Dur-ing labor we Would like	During labor we would like to avoid	During pushing and birth we would like to avoid	During pushing and birth we would like.	After birth for baby we would like

Breathing in labor

Laboring women can use breathing to promote relaxation or use it as a distraction. Many breathing techniques are not helpful for coping with labor pain, and they also put the mother at risk of hyperventilation. Breathing properly is essential for you.

If you want to understand breath work more properly it is recommended you try Prenatal yoga, during your Pregnancy.

Slow and abdominal breathing. Start with a deep relaxing sigh known as cleansing breath which releases all the tension from the body. In the nose, out of the mouth slowly.

Focus on breathing into the belly. Feeling the belly rise and fall with every breath.

Late active labor or transition breathing

A deep relaxing sigh. Long low moans or vocalizations. A deep relaxing sigh to the end.

Feather breathing to slow pushing

A deep relaxing sigh. Slow breathing, slow, in order to avoid hyperventilation a deep relaxing sigh at the end! Don't try to breathe uncomfortably, remember breath properly is breathing in a relaxed manner, environment, aliveness, truthfully, harmonically.

Relaxed breathing- Breathe in a relaxed manner, which means you relax fully, you cut out distractions,like phones and computers as much as you can, and you breathe fully. Enjoy your breathing, rather than breathing stressfully.

Enriching- Enriching means you breathe with enrichment, remembering you are rich, and content with little, with what you have, and yet determined to achieve quality lifestyle. Don't live in quantity lifestyle, live in quality, same goes for breathing.

Aliveness-Aliveness means you remember you are 'alive' so every moment you breathe, it is a gift of God, of grace and of witnessing another day of love. And you get to bring quality quality in the loving awareness presence of your breathing.

Environment– Pay attention to the environment where you are breathing, whether it's at work or home. notice your purpose there (means no need to poke nose everywhere, just do what you do the best!) and breathe joyfully, and be aware of toxins. remember every enviroment has some hidden toxins, (even if you have maintained it). Hence, be as aware as lovingly possible.

Hydrotherapy

Hydrotherapy can include both obvious use of shower or tub and subtle cold and warm compresses. It is a very effective comfort measure.

Showering in labor enhances labor progress as it creates physical comfort. The water flowing over the body increases tub and subtle and eases and relaxes the mother. The privacy and the shower also increases the release of endorphins and oxytocin. In addition, the stimulation of the shower on the belly can encourage contractions in a slow labor.

The tub or a Jacuzzi is a wonderful comfort measure. If a woman is having prodromal labor, resting in tub may allow her to sleep and possibly have slow contractions until she has rested. In active labor and transition, being in the water can enhance progress while reducing pain significantly. The tub is called the midwives epidural. Using hot and cold compress is very helpful.

For back pain, she can put the cold or hot compress, Give the expecting mother a nice oil massage.The reason is that it is difficult for a laboring mother to accept a cold pack after she has used heat, and using heat is infective if she uses it too early in labor.

Cold packs

Cool rice sock. Cool wet washcloth. Cold water bottle. Ice pack.

Where to use

Lower back for back labor. Back of the neck. Forehead, face, neck, upper chest.

Heat packs

Hot pack, hot wet towels in a folded chux pad.

What Are Birth Balls?

A birthing ball s a large-filled rubber ball that a woman can sit on during labor, A birthing ball allows the woman to rock back and forth seated over sofa or surface, a woman on a birthing ball may need support person to keep her steady. a birthing ball may be useful for labor'

Benefits of Birth Balls are Below:

It improves your posture and balance this helps your body to support the wieght of your pregnancy. It helps in increasing blood flow to your pelvic region it helps in opening your pelvic muscles. It helps to reduce your labor hours.

Post natal care

- After delivery the mother needs simple rest and sweet liquid juice for instant energy.
- Oiling and massage
- After placental removal, the mother is given twice the massage on her back and waist, this helps to reduce pain. Through massage on abdomen, helps the removal of all impurities from uterus.
- The woman who has just delivered should have,
- Juices
- Hot, fresh, nourishing easily digestible food (recommended during pregnancy as well)
- Coconut water
- Moong dal soup,
- Vegetable soup,
- And Sesame oil in cooking.
- Foods to be avoided.
- Chana dal, Urad dal, Bufflo milk, green peas,
- Cauliflower should be avoided immediately and should be eaten slowly.
- Spices, coriander seeds, fenugreek, Ajwain,
- Ginger should be used to the maximum

What to carry in my birth bag?

Labor /birth items.

- Massage tools.
- Lotion or massage oil

- Extra pillows with pillowcase
- Lip balm
- Hair accessories.
- Tennis balls
- Comfortable clothing.
- Toothbrush or toothpaste
- breath mints for mom
- Sour lollipops
- Hot/ cold pack
- Money
- Socks
- Robe and slippers
- Facial
- Orange peels(to hold if birth gets difficult
- Favorite childbirth book.

Postpartum items.

- Nursing bras.
- Clothes for mom and baby
- Phone list
- Car seat
- Blanket for baby.
- Personal hygiene items for mom and partners
- Diaper.

Some question answers to know about labor more accurately.

Most women lose their Mucus plug:

In the early labor. A mucus plug blocks the opening of the cervix to prevent bacteria from entering uterus. Before labor the mucus plug is expelled allowing the baby to pass during cervix, during labor and birth.

What happens during the third stage of labor

you deliver the placenta.

How long does early labor last?

Not more than 5 hours.

Crowning is when

Your baby's head starts to emerge. Once baby is out, your contractions will stop false.

Which hormone brings in contractions?

Oxytocin.

What are the four ps of labor?

Pitocin, powers, passage, psyche.

Benefits of massage in labor include?

It promotes relaxation, increases endorphins, it improves circulation.

Why is relaxation essential during pregnancy?

Relaxation during pregnancy is extremely effective coping mechanism in that it slows the body of the mother to be at more ease and free of intense tension.

What is the perineum?

The perineum is the soft skin between the anus and the vagina. Because of its proximity to where the baby exits the vaginal canal, as well as the pressure put on it while pushing, this delicate area is prone to tearing—especially for women having their first vaginal birth. During water birth the new born takes its first breath when the face is exposed to air.

What is nesting urge?

A sudden burst of desire to prepare for the babys arrival that may occur in early labor.

What is amniotic sac?

The fluid-filled sac that contains and protects fetus in the womb.

What is contraction?

Tightening of uterine muscle fibers that occur briefly throughout pregnancy, and more regularly and quickly during labor.

How small is a neonates head?

28-32 cm

What is the breaking of water by aritifical means known as?

Arom

The level of greatest severity of painful stimulation a person can endure is their?

Pain tolerance.

The device used to access fetal heart rate internally?

Fetal heart monitor

During water birth, the newborn takes its first breath when?

The babys lungs are filled with fluid at first, the baby takes its first breath whithin about 10 seconds after delivery, when exposed to air, and the caregiver gives a blow in its face, as the new borns central nervous system responds to change in temperature or enviroment.

Music to listen to during labor

Birds / Harp Relaxation / Do gentle stretches everyday.

To drink

Drink warm lukewarm water Red raspberry leaf tea.

To eat

Normal but in gentle quantities. Eat Chia seeds with water Iron, Eggs, tea and lemon water. Dried fruit nut mix bananas whole meal breads natural juices.

Food to avoid

Greasy fatty heavy foods fast foods..

Grace in Process Reflections

Over nurturing or under nurturing. Nurturing is a quality of the soul, when we over nurture we become an over giveer, but we should even learn to receive nurturing from others, our beautiful planet and each other.

A parent intuitively knows how and when to bond with the baby. That is a personal connection between you and the baby.

Holding longing

This wait for 9 months is ending, and the desire to hold your baby will intensify, relying on the comfort you can give and receive, practising breathing techniques would really help ease the mother.

We often wait to hold on to our truth knowing that we have to empty that space for us to hold it comfortably.

What improves the process loving actions toward each other and ourselves. Little thoughtful actions which mean the world to another person.

Looking foreward, and being hopeful

I expect the baby to be healthy every parent expects the baby to be Healthy. I expect the baby to have a good heart, Well If you do, its wise to release heavy expectations Of it and embrace the process the best way you can releasing heavy expectations and embracing light filled trust.

Since the time of harvesting Is near, whatever one sowed in the season and time of your pregnancy will, obviously reap now.

Beauty and happiness of birthing tears

Flowing from the ocean of memories and emotions, a part of you flows through your tear and is ready to be whole, and shown through your creation, the tear of joy hold it lovingly it is truly your treasure your emotion of pure love.

Bonding: Don't worry about bonding with the baby immediately, first the baby just needs basic physiological and medical attention and care.

I respect my emotions and will respect the emotions of my baby as well. To bring up an emotionally intelligent human being you have to be one yourself, starting with accepting, knowing when and how to express, keeping your presentation well, will project your emotions carefully forward or blaming anyone. Emotional intelligence creates a healthy foundation for a emotionally wise child.

Your emotions are on your side. Embrace them our emotions are truly our treasure's respecting them is a sign of an emotionally intelligent and emotionally available person.

During our pregnancy we are more emotionally avaialble than ever, we have to remember that if it feels good to be emotionally available those emotions are saved for your pregnancy and your private moments, allowing people you don't truly want to be intimate with in your emotional availability drains you. So respecting our emotional avaialbility is a sign of a emotionally healthy person isnt that true?

Persistently talking to random people. Not enjoying the moment just as it is. Not noticing how far you've come or someone else. Not aware of time/ day/ month not respecting someone else's emotional availability and time. I respect my own and others emotional availability when they are there.

A child is available to you for 9 months, a child gives us 9 months to understand emotional closeness. so make a habit of strengthening your emotional intelligence by remembering the above!

Twinkle Twinkle little child/girl/boy.
You are welcomed on earth,
By amazing delightful people,
Don't worry about a thing,
Just do your thing,
Your'e not far from our sight
We will take care of your youth
And wonder at your unique hood.
You are loved and hugged
Beyond you imagining,
Just keep smiling
And we want to
Respect your delicate light.

Poem written in 2013.

Inspired from twinkle Twinkle twinkle
little star

The human heart is one with the
Divine heart,
It beats not creating any chaos
But harmony in chaos,

It is reflected in
the glow of a newborns
face.

I respect my flow and glow
I respect my process,
Its safe to walk into labor now.

childs eyes
the innocent fresh eyes
lighten the presence of love in the world
with your love and light
there is hope.

Some times the child becomes
The reason for your days
Reason for your pains,
Reason of your joys
Reason which has reason
But just love,

However we cannot let our entire life be about
a child, that is unhealthy, but it.
it can be a loving equal connection then it is
filled with
So much joy!

We cant define our self worth by having a baby, we are a unique individual ourselves, so will be our child, many women or even men feel unequal to their partners and this obviously does not make the process easy, so trusting that a woman's journey through labor is the families labor of love the process is where the true help shows, after all it is all in the quality behind the scene work, which bring about the positive fruitful result which is good. So, one has to just make sure that process is going damage free and with care faith and trust.

Message to the reader

This chapter as it was the end had to be on the labor of love and all the behind the scene work required to make a healthy and a gorgeous baby. This chapter also talks about some recipes to cook for the mother the poems in the end were obviously written by me, and even the umbilical cord connection, when I said that the baby's navel connects to yours, I meant the harmonious connection we can experience when our babies after they are born, the umbilical cord also connects to the navel of the baby showing how important is that center development for the baby, without the navel and the heart the entire baby's growth is not possible, being a healer and an intuitive I felt this made sense and I added it in the book the end lines the human heart is one with the divine heart, I wrote in the end, was actually written a little long ago. You must have crossed through, divine timing poem and the month awareness poems in the beginning. when there is a beautiful message to be shared structure truly guides and helps. And I think it structured quite well and I am great full I hope you enjoyed reading this chapter. Well also all the medical information is well researched and studied before adding in here, as I am also studying a Child Birth Educator Program from Mumbai.

Meaning of intention: what someone intends or plans to do.

Activity and contemplation for you.

• Can you make it a soft intention every month, to go through your day, intuitively, looking back with wonder and respect, looking at the present with awe and gratitude, and looking ahead gracefully and with anticipation?

• What was the most endearing part of being pregnant?

• If you are interested in being a childbirth educator, or any of the related programs, you must google and find your source, there are so many I am currently doing from 'Cappa' which is an international organization for these certifications.

Quote to ponder: Where there is graceful hope, there are also miracles

These are some excerpts from my future works.

Wish come true

What would you do if your wish came true?
You would see Good.
You would see god
You would feel peace
you would be grace

you would send a silent blessing to
someone's day,
you would be helpful
you would be ok with others being helped too
you would connect gently.
You would not judge or condemn,
But find a creative solution to a problem.

A song written By me.
My soul was searching for a rainbow,
Then I saw the colors of you,
I met so many,
But my favorite one was you.
When I saw you,
I knew you were the one,
I have been seeking on,
So, I said yes
To you me and what
We could become.
The rainbow in you
Shines so wonderfully tonight.
So lets make this bright,
And make this culture right,
Than yesterday,
And be proud of this day.

The busy bee's

Do you know bees like to sleep on flowers and hold each others feet? Do you know why they hold each others feet? While each other sleep? to tell each other, I respect your presence in my life, and your journey, and I am there for you , you don't have to do all the work alone!

Bees work together like a team, they make honey, and that's all they do, sometimes we wouldn't wonder nature would not do anything essential only by its itself, we all need each other!

Notes

1. What were some of the favourite lines from this chapter. How did it make you Feel?

_____

_____

_____

_____

_____

_____

_____

_____

2. What insights did you receive to make your experience more enriching and meaningful?

_____

_____

_____

_____

_____

_____

_____

_____

Bibliography

- Waiting for baby. A day by day countdown to your baby's birth.

- If the Buddha had kids, Charlotte, Kasl. Phd.

- Sweet baby touch, the infant massage book. Sharon Melvin.

- The book of balance Lex Gonzales.pt.

- The art of Lactation, Jennifer Elizabeth, Maiden.

- Fang shui mommy Bailey Gaddis,

- Child of mine- Ellen scatter.

- The nourishing tradition book of baby and child care- Sally Follen Morell and Thomas.s Cowen.

- Paintings By Neha Ajmera (jaipur), Amar Singh (jaipur) and Jai ranjit (mumbai).

Recommended Reading

- On pregnancy and parenting.

- Magical beginnings, Enchanted lives, Deepak Chopra.

- 100 promises to my baby- Mallika Chopra

- Spiritual pregnancy- Gopika kapoor

- Roots and wings- Raksha Bharadia.

- Conscious parenting- Shefali Tsbary.

- If Buddha had kids- Charlotte Kasl.

- Just breathe - Mallika Chopra

- The nourishing tradition for baby and child care-
  Sally Falcon Morellos

- Sweet baby touch - Sharon Melvin.

- Fang shui mommy - Bailey Gaddis.

- How to breastfeed twins without losing your mind-
  Elizabeth Malloy

- Caring for children and toddlers with attachment
  difficulties- Chris Taylor

- The art of lactation - Jennifer Elizabeth

- The book of Balance - lex Gonzales

- Yummy mummy- Karishma kapoor.

- How to declutter with archangel Jophiel -zz.Rae

- Pregnancy the complete childbirth book - Nutan pundit.

- The mindful mother- naomi Chunilal

- Kids music and autism - Dorita.s berger

- Spiritual secrets of pregnancy and Birth -Dr Tushar

- How mothers love and how relationships are born - Naomi Staden.

- Health books.Perfect health - deepak Chopra.

- Ageless body timeless mind- deepak chopra

- You can heal your life _ Louise hay

- Transformation story of a bird: GL sampoorna.

- Spiritual health

- God speaks: Meher baba.

- The power of now : Eckhart tolle.

- The monk who sold his ferari: Robin Sharma.

- Women food and god: Ganeen roth.

- Living with special abilities: Afroze Jahan.

- Women of the elements: Rashmi anand.

- Yoga for easier pregnancy and birth : Anjali dec.

- A to Z for back pain: Dr Shiv dua.

- Mindful leader: Micheal bunting.

- Weight loss a rocket science : Dr Sunny Bawa.

Happiness is when you realise your children turned out to be humane, and very good people. The best kind of nurturing given to children is spiritual nurturing, and sometimes even from children to parents.

Perfectionism is hard to achieve, understanding is easier'

Wish you a wise and a Joyfilled Ending!

www.ingramcontent.com/pod-product-compliance
Lightning Source LLC
Chambersburg PA
CBHW050922030726
47503CB00007BB/2429